TOM ANGLEBERGER

AMULET BOOKS
LONDON

Cataloging-in-Publication Data has been applied for and may be obtained from the Library of Congress.

ISBN: 978-1-4197-1355-2

Text copyright © 2014 Tom Angleberger
Book design by Melissa J. Arnst

Printed and bound in U.S.A.
10 9 8 7 6 5 4 3 2 1

THE ART OF BOOKS SINCE 1949
The Market Building
72-82 Rosebery Avenue
London, UK EC1R 4RW
www.abramsbooks.co.uk

THIS BOOK IS DEDICATED TO LAURA
AND JASON, WITH GRATITUDE FOR ALL
THEY'VE DONE TO AID THE REBELLION!

THE ORIGAMI REBEL ALLIANCE!

TOMMY + FOLDY-WAN

KELLEN (ME!) + LUKE

SARA + CHEWIE
+ HAN F.

HARVEY + ANAKIN

AMY + R2D2

LANCE + C3PO

QUAVONDO + KIT FISTO

MURKY + PAD-MÉ

JAMES + HANDO C.

REMI + MARA + EWOKS
+ ARM SOCKS

JEN + VENTRESS

YODA (BUT NOT DWIGHT!)

(PLUS MIKE + MACE . . . HOPEFULLY!)

TO: MS. RABBSKI

FROM: PRINCESS LABELMAKER

I HAVE STOLEN THE REBELS' SECRET CASE FILE.

IT CONTAINS INFORMATION VITAL TO OUR SURVIVAL.

AND NOW I AM GIVING IT TO YOU.

BUT I AM NO TRAITOR.

I AM SHOWING YOU THE FILE BECAUSE I THINK IT

WILL MAKE YOU UNDERSTAND US BETTER.

BUT THEY WOULD BE SOOOO MAD IF THEY FOUND OUT.

SO MY IDENTITY MUST BE A SECRET. THAT IS WHY I

AM USING A LABELMAKER TO WRITE TO YOU. ALSO, IT

IS COOL.

PLEASE READ THIS CASE FILE. AND THEN I TRUST

YOU WILL JOIN US. NOT FIGHT US.

HELP US, PRINCIPAL RABBSKI . . . YOU ARE OUR

ONLY HOPE . . .

THE FUNTIME MENACE

BY TOMMY

I can't believe we're having to make ANOTHER case file about fighting FunTime! I thought we'd have won by now . . . but it just won't die! (Kind of like Darth Maul!)

And now that it's April, it almost seems like it's too late to fix the problem this year.

A few weeks ago, Rabbski told our parents she would try to do something . . . but she hasn't. We just keep on watching FunTime videos and filling out worksheets to PREP-are for the stupid state Standards tests.

ROBOT LEGS

I'LL FRY MY BEST. OOPS, I MEAN 'TRY'

EMPRESS RABBSKI

And those tests are coming up in May, and then school will be over. True, it will be awesome to get a break from watching the evil Professor FunTime and his even more evil singing calculator, Gizmo.

But the thing is . . . if we, the Origami Rebel Alliance, don't beat it this year, then it'll just be back next year! And that will mean a whole new year of taking PREP classes and watching the Professor instead of taking the classes we actually like, like art and band and chorus and LEGO robots.

So that's why we have our big rebel plan, which right now doesn't seem to be doing much.

We threatened Rabbski that if she didn't dump FunTime and give us our classes and field trip back, we would do really, really bad on the state Standards test on purpose. She flipped out, of course, and told us how important those tests are and how taking

SARLACC PIT

them is a law and how we were "disrupting the learning environment" and everything like that.

We all SAID we were going to do it anyway . . . but I think actually most people are going to chicken out.

I know that I would LIKE to chicken out. It's scary to be a rebel!

But when I told Origami Yoda how I might chicken out, he said, "Chicken out do not."

That's easy for him to say! Origami Yoda isn't actually a student under the authority of Principal Rabbski! Dwight—who IS a student under the authority of Ms. Rabbski—DID chicken out! Somehow he's out but his finger puppet is in! Is that possible? Apparently so!

"But it's scary!" I said. "Every time I see Rabbski, she glares at me. I keep expecting her to call *me* a 'disruption to the learning environment' and try to kick me out of school like she did you, Dwight. And I'm sure she's

OUT →

← IN

MMM . . . EVIL!

cooking up some kind of plan to destroy us once and for all."

"Hrmmm . . . ," Origami Yoda said, "maybe plan she does have . . . but fear not. That is why you have Foldy-Wan . . . to be fearless when fear all around you is."

Uh . . . fear is going to be all around me? I'm going to be surrounded by fear?

I sincerely hope that doesn't happen, because I don't know that I CAN be fearless.

Anyway, I guess we'll find out what happens as we put this case file together.

Previous case files have answered questions like, Is Origami Yoda real? Will Darth Paper take Harvey to the Dark Side? Can the Fortune Wookiee save us AND Dwight? And can we find a way to fight FunTime?

We did find a way—creating the Origami Rebellion. But now we're just sort of stuck.

So I hope this case file ends up answering the question, How did the rebels beat Fun-Time?

HARVEY'S ORIGAMI REBEL ALLIANCE INSIGNIA

(slightly squashed*)

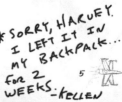

* SORRY, HARVEY. I LEFT IT IN MY BACKPACK... FOR 2 WEEKS. —KELLEN

5

And not, How did Rabbski beat the rebels?

Or, How did Tommy get transferred to CREF, the "alternative" school for learning disrupters?

OR, How much did it hurt when our brains shriveled up from FunTime-induced boredom?

SHRIVELED ➙ ∞

Harvey's Comment

My brain shriveled up a long time ago, remember? I have scientific evidence (sort of).

What I want to know is, when is Rabbski going to actually do something? She promised our parents she would talk to the school board and try to find a solution. Well, they can't be trying very hard, because every day we come back to school and nothing has changed and we have to go watch a dumb video and then do a test-prep worksheet.

I don't want to alarm anyone, but every worksheet is pushing origami Anakin closer to the Dark Side!

origami Anakin says, "We were fools to trust Empress Rabbski! She isn't using this time to set us free . . . she's building a better trap!"

My Comment: Sometimes I think the same thing!

I hate to say this, but Origami Yoda seems to be wrong. He thinks Rabbski may have some goodness in her, but as far as I can tell, she is still the enemy. Why else does she continue making us watch FunTime EVERY DAY?

WRONG?

PROFESSOR FUNTIME + GIZMO

AS I SAID,

I DONT THINK YOU ARE THE REAL ENEMY. THAT'S WHY I

FUNTIME REVISITED

BY PROFESSOR FUNTIME

AND GIZMO

HAD TO GO AGAINST THE REST OF THE REBELS. THIS

CHAPTER WILL SHOW YOU WHO THE REAL ENEMY IS.

Tommy's note: In case anyone here has forgotten how bad FunTime is, I present an actual scene from FunTime, transcribed by me and illustrated by Kellen.

Professor FunTime: Guess what, Gizmo.

Gizmo: What's that, Professor FunTime?

Professor FunTime: Today we're going to take a tough problem and break it down into easy steps!

Gizmo: Did somebody say "BREAK IT DOWN"?

[Electronic drumbeat starts.]

[Professor FunTime starts doing that horsey dance from "Gangnam Style."]

Professor FunTime: [rapping] A problem is presented to me: Fifty-seven divided by ninety-three. I know I'll need to go into decimal— Draw a dot! Add a zero! Now it's ninety-three into five seventy.

Gizmo: OPPA FUNTIME STYLE!

[Yes, they worked out the entire problem this way . . .]

Professor FunTime: [wearing sunglasses] Point six-one-two!

Gizmo: [also wearing sunglasses] Yeah . . . that's FUNTIME STYLE!

Professor FunTime: HEYYYYY, S—

The TV went silent.

"Jabba the Puppett just pressed the mute button," said Mr. Howell. "Anyone got a problem

z z z z z

with that? Good. The silence is pleasing to Jabba the Puppett. Now, do the fleeping worksheets in silence, too."

Harvey's Comment

I can't believe I'm saying this, but I WISH I was in Mr. Howell's class. Ms. Puckett refuses to turn down the volume at all! I had to listen to the whole song!

My Comment: Actually, now that we have the sound off every day for FunTime, I find myself wondering what new terrible songs they've come up with. Can they outdo themselves and actually get worse?

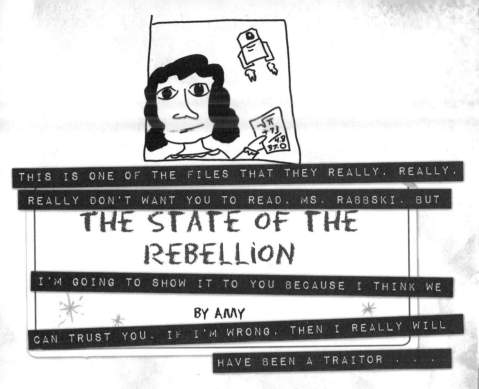

THE STATE OF THE REBELLION

BY AMY

Tommy, here are the numbers you asked for:

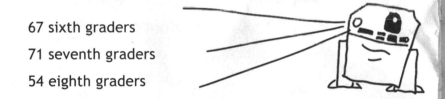

67 sixth graders

71 seventh graders

54 eighth graders

R2 and I would be a lot happier if we could get more people to sign up. The more people who sign up, the easier it will be to Blow Up The Test.

Remember, the current plan is for everybody to try to score a 70 on the test. That way they'll pass

GOOD NAME FOR A PET RANCOR.

and Rabbski won't be able to hold them back a grade, which I think was an empty threat, anyway!

By getting a 70 instead of their normal score of, say, 85, they will drag down the school average a tiny bit. And that tiny bit will lower the average just enough to make the whole SCHOOL fail.

Rabbski is so scared of that happening that she's been willing to bargain with us.

But what she doesn't know is that our plan might not work!

I worry that a lot of our so-called rebels are going to chicken out and either do their "best on the test" or at least do pretty good, just to be on the safe side. So they might get an 80 instead of a 70.

Well, when R2 ran those numbers, he let out one of his sad whistles! That would drag down the average . . . but not enough!!! Instead of Blowing Up The Test, that would be like when that first X-wing drops the torpedo on the Death Star and says, "Negative! It didn't go in. Just impacted on the surface."

We either need braver rebels who are willing to take a big risk . . . or MORE regular rebels. If we had

12

EXHAUST PORT

IMPACT

everyone in the school join us, they could all miss just one or two questions and we would still Blow Up The Test.

But as you know, we've already asked everybody in the school we can think of. And we've been bugging some of them a little too much about it, and they just tell us to shut up.

So we need every new member we can get . . . I just don't know where we're going to get them.

Harvey's Comment

Son of a mynock! I didn't realize the numbers were so bad!

Well, you can count on me to get EXACTLY 70 points. I expect to know every answer on that test. I'll get the first 70 right and the last 30 wrong. No problem!

My Comment: I wish I had that kind of confidence. I have to admit, I was sort of planning to aim for 75 or 80 to be on the safe side. Math isn't really my best subject. Believe it or not, I actually considered paying

MYNOCK

SON OF A MYNOCK!

attention to FunTime so I would know how to do all the problems so I could make sure my score was as low as possible without failing. But then when I tried to watch, it was so intensely boring and pointless that when it was over, I felt like I knew LESS than when I started.

Kellen's Comment

ANYONE ELSE NOTICE THAT THE INITIALS OF "BLOW UP THE TEST" ARE B.U.T.T.?

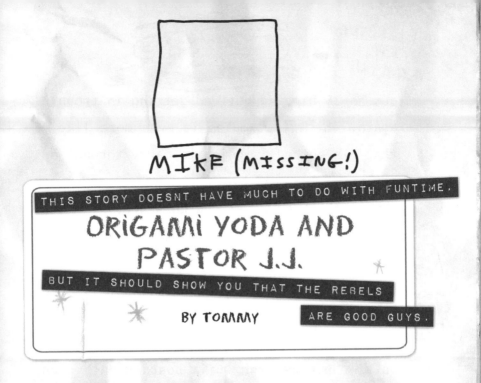

MIKE (MISSING!)

ORIGAMI YODA AND PASTOR J.J.

BY TOMMY

Regardless of what happens with Rabbski and FunTime, we need to rescue Mike.

Mike is still "missing." His mother found out about Origami Yoda seeing the future and making predictions, and she got worried that it was somehow connected to devil worship or cults. She won't let him be part of the Origami Rebel Alliance, talk to Origami Yoda or us, or even use his Mace Windu puppet. That really stinks, because Mace Windu really was helping him not flip out all the time. So

HUH? I DON'T EVEN LIKE STAR WARS!

I ♥ Justin Beiber

THIS STINKS!

MACE

FLIPPING OUT AGAIN →

now he IS flipping out and getting in trouble again, which just makes it even more likely that his mother is going to carry through on her threat to pull him out of school and send him to the Lighthouse church school with his cousins.

PLASTIC OUIJA

I remember now that back in the fourth grade Lance had a sleepover and we played with a Ouija board, and later Mike's mom found out and was furious. (Which was really unfair, because the Ouija board didn't even work.)

Anyway, she's really religious and she doesn't like stuff like that.

So I asked Origami Yoda how we can stop her.

"Faith a precious thing is. Interfere we must not," said Origami Yoda.

"I don't want him to stop going to church or anything," I said. "I just want his mom to change her mind . . ."

"Hrmmm . . . ," said Origami Yoda. "Perhaps

do something we may . . . We must turn to . . . Pastor J.J.!"

"Pastor J.J.? Dude, Mike's preacher is nuts. I've seen him in action! At first you think he's just this goofy guy with crazy ties and a weird haircut. Then when he starts preaching, he gets all crazy and starts yelling about demons and stuff."

"Ties of craziness?" asked Origami Yoda.

"Uh, yeah," I said. "He wears crazy ties, but—"

"New tie we must buy him," said Origami Yoda.

"Why should I buy him a tie?" I asked. "What does that have to do with anything???"

"Dude," said Kellen, "where have you been for the last year? Origami Yoda has looked into the way all things are interconnected and seen that a new tie will change Mike's destiny. Stop arguing, shut up, and buy the tie!"

"Fine," I said. "What kind of tie?"

Origami Yoda told me exactly what kind of tie to get and I almost started to think I could see the interconnectedness of all things, too.

THIS IS THE TIE YOU ARE LOOKING FOR...

But then I went online and saw that the tie cost thirty-two bucks plus shipping, and I almost freaked out. But I looked at Foldy-Wan, and he seemed to be telling me to buy the tie, too.

I entered the address of Mike's church and paid extra for fast shipping. (So, by the way, all the rest of you rebels owe me four dollars each so I can pay my parents back for using their credit card!)

Now we can only wait and see what happens.

Harvey's Comment

I'm not giving you four dollars. And what kind of tie was it, anyway?

My Comment: I'll tell you . . . for four dollars.

MIKE (BACK)

I'M BACK IN!!!

BY MIKE!!!!!!!!!!!!

IT EVEN WORKED! AND LOOK . . .

You're not going to believe this, but . . . everything is okay again!

This morning in church, Pastor J.J. was wearing a YODA tie!

Yoda, right there on his tie!

I made Mom ask him about it, and he said, "Oh, yeah, isn't this a great tie? It just showed up here at the church."

"Well," said Mom, "we asked because we've been a little concerned about *Star Wars* lately . . . Not quite sure it's a good thing for Mike."

JUDGE
ME
BY
MY
TIES
DO
YOU?

"A good thing? It's a great thing! *Star Wars* is the greatest parable since *The Pilgrim's Progress*. You've got your good, your evil, your Light Side, your Dark Side . . ."

And basically he launched into a mini sermon about how great *Star Wars* is, right there in the narthex! I couldn't believe it.

When Mom said she was worried because of Origami Yoda, Pastor J.J. actually got me to fold him one! (I did an emergency five-fold Yoda out of the church bulletin.) He loved it.

"But they've actually been taking advice from this thing," Mom said.

"Well, better Yoda than Darth Vader! Right, Mike?"

"Right!" I said.

When we got home, Mom gave me all my *Star Wars* movies and stuff back, and she actually sat down and watched *A New Hope* with me! Can you believe she had never seen it? She LOVED IT!

Anyway . . . Give me the Holocron notebook, because I'm back, and so is Mace Windu!

Harvey's Comment

I'm still not giving Tommy four dollars.

My Comment: Big surprise.

AMY

AMY AND R2 (AND LANCE AND C-3PO, I GUESS) CONFRONT RABBSKI

BY AMY

"This is an outrage!" I said at lunch one day after we had been forced to watch a particularly stupid episode of FunTime. It was a review episode . . . Uh, okay . . . FunTime IS a review. So this was a review of the review? Uh, okay . . . But did we really need to hear "FunTime Style" again?

"I can't take any more," I said. "We need to ask Rabbski what's going on."

"But she said she would work on it," somebody whimpered.

"Yeah," I said. "She said that three weeks ago at

LET'S REVIEW!

the meeting with our parents! And since then, what have we STILL been doing every day?"

The answer was FunTime, obviously.

Every. Single. Day.

As Lance would say, "WHUT THE HUTT?"

It was like she had just forgotten our Jabba-powered victory at the meeting with our parents. She had promised us—AND our parents—that she was going to talk to the school board about finding some way out of this FunTime mess.

And yet nothing changed.

And our so-called Rebellion was just sitting there taking it. Now I know why R2-D2 is beeping all the time! He's tired of waiting. He was ready to take down the Death Star on day one.

"If none of you are going to go talk to her, I am!" I said. "She's right over there on the other side of the cafeteria. C'mon, Lance, we're going!"

"Why do I have to go?"

"Because C-3PO is a protocol droid. We may need some fancy talking."

"Uh . . ."

"Great. Real fancy. Now, let's go."

But it turned out that there wasn't much talking at all. Here's what Rabbski said: "Working on it! Should have some news for you soon . . ."

Then she rushed off like she had something really important to do. Yeah, right.

LUKE SKYFOLDER FLUNKS LANGUAGE ARTS

BY KELLEN

Okay, this all started when I got my book report back from Ms. Bolton. She gave me a B-, then scratched it out and gave me an incomplete: because she said a comic book isn't a book!

So I went up after class and showed her *Fangbone* and pointed out that it has 128 pages, which really makes it a graphic novel and not what people normally think of by the term "comic book."

"Nice try, Kellen," she said, like I was

FANGBONE #3: BIRTHDAY PARTY OF DREAD
IS A GREAT BOOK!

KELLEN CAMPBELL

LANGUAGE ARTS 2

PERIOD 5

THE PROTAGONIST, FANGBONE, IS INVITED TO A LITTLE KID'S BIRTHDAY PARTY. BUT THE ANTAGONIST, A WIZARD, SHOWS UP AND CAUSES STUFF TO COME TO LIFE. THEN THAT STUFF ATTACKS FANGBONE AND HIS FRIEND AND THE LITTLE KIDS AT THE PARTY. THE FUNNY THING IS THE LITTLE KIDS THINK IT'S ALL PART OF THE PARTY, AND THE MOM KEEPS MISSING EVERYTHING. ALSO, THE WIZARD PUT A MARK ON FANGBONE'S FRIEND SO NOW THE CRUSHA WANTS TO KILL HIM, AND THAT ALL HAPPENS AT THE SCIENCE FAIR.

FANGBONE #3 IS A MAN VS. MAN STORY, ALTHOUGH TECHNICALLY IT'S MAN VS. DROOL, THE EVIL SORCERER. AND TECHNICALLY IT'S JUST DROOL'S BIG TOE.

THE AUTHOR IS NAMED MICHAEL REX AND THE BOOK WAS PUBLISHED IN 2012.

IN CONCLUSION, MICHAEL REX HAS WRITTEN ANOTHER GREAT FANGBONE BOOK!

B-   *Incomplete! Kellen, I just discovered online that "Fangbone" is a comic book. Please see me after class to choose an ACTUAL BOOK for your book report.*
      —Ms. Bolton

trying to play a trick or something. "Now, I want you to go to the library as soon as possible and pick out a new book. Bring it back here so I can approve it. Then you'll need to read it and write a new book report before I can give you a grade. Otherwise, it will be a zero, which could bring your six-weeks grade down to an F."

Well, last year I found out what happens when I get an F on a report card. My mother freaked out and to calm her down my dad suggested a huge punishment and then my mother doubled the punishment and when I complained she said, "Oh, if this ever happens again, you'll find out what a REAL punishment is. Right, Tyler?" And she looked at my big brother and he was like, "Yes, ma'am," because he hadn't watched TV, been on a date, or driven his car since November.

Mom

TYLER

So, basically, I had no choice. I knew it was unfair, but I couldn't risk getting an F. So I slunk away and figured I'd try to get away with reading the shortest "real book" I could find.

But when I was putting *Fangbone* back in my backpack, I saw Luke Skyfolder in there . . .

I thought about how Luke just wouldn't give up in *The Empire Strikes Back*. Darth Vader keeps reaching out to him and Luke just keeps shaking his head. Eventually you want Luke to say yes just so he can climb off of that thing to safety. But he keeps saying, "No! I'll never join you! Never!"

So I decided not to write a new book report. I decided to write this . . .

WELL, ACTUALLY MANY OF THE MONTHLY ISSUES COMMONLY CALLED "COMIC BOOKS" ARE ACTUALLY JUST CHAPTERS . . .

WILLY THE WALKING WAFFLE! #4
NIGHT OF THE WAFFLPIRE!

BUT WHEN ALL THE CHAPTERS OF A STORY ARC ARE COLLECTED INTO A GRAPHIC NOVEL THEN YOU HAVE A BOOK !!!

THE WAFFLE CHRONICLES

BUT COMIC BOOKS ARE JUST SUPERHEROES BEATING EACH OTHER UP.

WRONG!!!!

COMIC BOOKS ARE ABOUT ALL KINDS OF THINGS:

SMILE

CHI

BAKE SALE

BESIDES, IF A FAMOUS WRITER WROTE A BOOKS ABOUT A SUPER HERO, THAT WOULD STILL BE A BOOK, RIGHT?

RIGHT!

THE ODYSSEY BY HOMER

Before I handed it in to Ms. Bolton, I showed it to Lance and Murky.

Lance said, "First of all: Stooky!"

"Agreed!" said Murky.

"Second of all," said Lance, "I think you need a little help from a protocol droid."

He held up C-3PO.

"May I suggest that you have a backup plan, sir?"

"Like what?"

"A proper book report, if you take my meaning, sir."

"No. Weren't you listening? I decided not to give in to Ms. Bolton! I'll take my F if I have to!"

"It is not Ms. Bolton that worries me . . . if you take my meaning, sir."

"Huh?"

"He means your mom," said Murky.

"Yeah," said Lance. "When Ms. Bolton throws this in the trash and gives you an F—which she will—your mom is going to say you were

being lazy. Show your mom a 'real book' book report and she'll see this wasn't about you trying to get out of an assignment. It'll prove you were really standing up for something."

So I checked out this book called *Revenge of the Shipless Pirates*. It was okay, but not as good as *Fangbone*. But I wrote a report about it.

Then I turned in the manifesto to Ms. Bolton.

She didn't throw it in the trash. But she barely glanced over it before she gave it back and said she was disappointed that I couldn't follow simple instructions. And she looked in her grade book and said I would be getting an F for the six weeks and she hoped I didn't do anything so foolish during the final six weeks, because now my grade for the whole year was looking bad.

DUH!

But C-3PO was right. After I told my parents—and after my dad got my mom calm enough to listen to me—she read my *Shipless*

Pirates report and reduced my punishment from six months without TV to two months. That is an improvement . . . BUT these two months are when all the season finales happen!

Now Luke has to shout "NOOO!" again and jump into the Cloud City air-conditioning system . . .

Harvey's Comment

My fear is that without TV to watch, Kellen is going to have more time to draw comics.

My Comment: Good grief, Harvey! No wonder Kellen draws you in your underwear all the time!

Anyway, I'm glad I have Miss Bauer. She says we can do book reports on graphic novels as long as we take them seriously and don't just zip through them. So far this year, I've done reports on *Smile, Amulet, Sidekicks,* and *The Donner Dinner Party* (which I also used as a source for a history report).

NOOOOOO! IT CAN'T BE TRUE !!! I NEVER MISS DOCTOR WHO! NEVER!!!

JEN + VENTRESS

PAD-MÉ ORIGAMIDALA AND THE UGLIEST SHOES IN THE WORLD

BY JEN

Tommy, I can't believe I'm writing another big e-mail to you! My boyfriend is going to get jealous! (Not that that matters, since I'm dumping him soon, anyway.)

You probably haven't noticed, but McQuarrie Middle School has been going through Boot Mania lately. Everybody—every girl, at least—is wearing DotDotBoots from Highway. (Highway is that store at the mall that my dumb boyfriend won't even go into because it's "wall-to-wall girl clothes and big-eyed teddy bears.")

DotDotBoots are WAY too expensive, but just about everyone has at least one pair, and one of the other

DOT
DOT
BOOT

♪ I'M GOING ON A BEAR HUNT, A BEAR ♪ HUNT, A BEAR HUNT...

cheerleaders, Raina, has eleven pairs! I have three pairs and I bought two of those with gift cards after Christmas, and by the way, I bought them BEFORE they got super-popular, because I actually liked them. (In case you're wondering, I got the purple ones with pink fur and the green-orange striped ones with white fur.)

I knew they were mega-popular when even Melodee bought some. She normally only wears LollyHops.

Anyway, you remember that girl Lisa? The one who had that smelliness problem? Well, she doesn't have that problem anymore, which I know because she sits across the aisle from me and Melodee on the bus. She doesn't talk much, but one day—after Melodee got off—she said, "Why does everyone keep asking me about my shoes?"

I looked down at her feet . . . and I saw the Ugliest Shoes in the World! They looked SORT OF like DotDotBoots, but they weren't. They were just wrong. They were all wrinkly and the fur looked diseased. And they didn't look like the right size . . . They were all clonky and horrible. They reminded me of something—not a shoe, but I didn't know what.

ARTIST'S
RECREATION →

"Uh," I said, sort of in shock. "What are they?"

"That's what everybody keeps asking me," said Lisa. "They're from Cranky's Flea Market. I thought these are what everybody wears."

"Er . . . no, not exactly."

"Where did you get yours?"

"Highway."

"Oh, okay," she said. "Maybe I'll check that out . . ."

She sort of faded out and started messing with her backpack.

Well, here's the thing: I knew that she knew that Highway is super-expensive, and I don't mean to be mean, but I just don't think she could afford real DotDotBoots. I mean, I could only afford them because of the gift cards and—again, not to be mean—I don't think Lisa's family has that kind of money, and she probably doesn't have two awesome aunts who send her gift cards like I do.

It seemed unfair, and it seemed even more unfair the next day when I heard Brianna laughing about Lisa's "butt boots." (Although I did realize that's what they had reminded me of.)

I remembered how you guys all chipped in to buy

WOW, SHE'S NASTY!

Mike's preacher that tie. That gave me the idea to have everyone chip in to buy Lisa some boots.

But then that would be REALLY *awkward* when we tried to give them to her. I even thought about getting a gift card and slipping it in her locker. But I was pretty sure she would know where it came from, and that would be *awkward*, too.

Later in the library, me and Sara and Amy all talked about it, but we didn't come up with anything. All R2-D2 would tell me was "beep." And Sara's Fortune Wookiee said, "GRULPHHHH," which Han Foldo said meant, "'Wookiees don't wear boots.' And I only wear black ones, kid."

And of course my puppet, Ventress, has got The. Worst. Fashion. Sense. Ever. (What is up with those weird shirts with triangles cut out of them? She is such an awesome character, but she seriously needs better clothes!)

So then we asked Origami Yoda, and he said, "Boots what are?"

"You know . . . boots!" I said. "Like on your feet."

"Feet I have not."

I hadn't noticed that before . . . but he DOESN'T have feet!

Anyway, I explained the whole thing to him, and he said, "Hrmmm . . . Uncertain fashion is. Always in motion . . ."

"ARRGH!" I said. "Will someone please take this seriously?"

"Queen Amidala . . . takes fashion seriously she does."

So . . . we found Murky and Lance flopping around near the magazines.

"What are you guys doing?" I asked them.

"Practicing leaning on air," said Lance, like it was something a normal person might do. Sometimes I wonder how Amy ended up with such a weird boyfriend. (Better than my boring jerkface one, though!)

Anyway, we explained the whole thing, and Murky got out Queen Pad-mé Origamidala. And she said, "It's simple. You have the power to make her butt boots popular."

"How?"

"Well, on Naboo I made these crazy hats popular."

"Oh, I thought those were, like, traditional costumes," said Sara.

"No, I just liked them," said Pad-mé. "And once I wore them, my people chose to wear funny hats, too!"

"So you mean . . . ?"

"Yes," said Pad-mé. "You, Jen, are the princess of this school. Whatever you choose to wear is what your people will wear. Why do you think all the girls are wearing DotDotBoots?"

"Because of me?"

"Exactly. So . . . lead the way, Princess Jen! Get yourself some of these butt boots and suddenly Lisa will be the second most fashionable girl in school."

"It shall be so," I said. "Butt boots for all my people! Um . . . well, for all the girl people!"

It made sense. So that weekend I got my dad to drive me and Melodee over to Cranky's. I had never been there before. Man, that place is JACKED UP! There are some weird people there selling really weird stuff. I think it would be Ventress's favorite place: She could buy new outfits and new weapons in one stop!

MELODEE

UH . . . NO THANKS

At first we couldn't find the butt boots. Then we found out they were in the parking lot out back, where people sell stuff out of their cars.

The guy selling them was this really, really old man with a cigar, an oxygen tank with a hose running up to his nose, and a trailer full of butt boots and wrenches.

All the butt boots were exactly the same—same size (too big), same color (peach), with really, really fake-looking fur that was also peach but somehow didn't really match. And they had tags that said "Genuine DotDotBoots," so I guess that's how Lisa got confused.

A sign said: $5 A PAIR/WRENCH OR 5 PAIRS/WRENCHES FOR $20.

We bought five. (My dad bought five wrenches and was SO happy about it!) Then we had churros from the churro truck. Not only did they taste great, but we had a lightsaber fight with them before we ate them, and Melodee's broke after two seconds and she ended up getting chocolate-goo filling all over herself. She should have known better than to mess with me and Ventress!

On Monday me, Melodee, Sara, Amy, and Cassie all wore them. Weirdly, they were really comfortable. But they did look like butts.

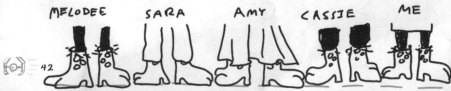

MELODEE   SARA   AMY   CASSIE   ME

Lisa wasn't wearing hers that first day. But she must have noticed us, because she wore hers the rest of the week after that!

And then, Raina started wearing them, too! And her boyfriend, Roman, said they looked "hot," which means he's either dumber or smarter than I thought.

So now they are definitely a "hot" item at McQuarrie, and I bet that old weird guy is going to sell out!

We did it, gang! YAY!

Harvey's Comment

I can't comment because I fell asleep after the first sentence. But . . . yay, I guess?

My Comment: Wow, that was a lot of information about boots. I guess the reason it's important to this case file is that it gives us that picture of Murky standing around with a Queen Origamidala puppet on his finger willingly talking about girls' shoes. That's Murky and . . . well . . . that's sort of what the next chapter is all about.

RHONDELLA

RHONDELLA-BUT NOT AHSOKA-AND THE CLASS PHOTO

BY KELLEN AND LANCE

Well, the first we knew that anything was going on was when we noticed that Murky was acting kind of depressed.

Usually he is like a toddler who can't handle artificial colors and has just had an orange soda. You know, kind of wired on happy juice.

WARNING LABEL! "CAUTION: MAKES KIDS WIG OUT."

But now it was like he was on straight tap water. Basically, he was more likely to say "nostrul" than "stooky," if you know what I mean. But the weird thing was, he wasn't saying either "nostrul" or "stooky," he was just keeping quiet and not being his usual awesome self.

STOOKY!

nostrul

And he was wearing really boring clothes instead of the neon, hurt your eyeballs stuff he usually wears.

We didn't know why, and when we asked, he got all huffy.

I (Kellen) tried to ask his sister about it on the bus. (She's still in elementary school, but our bus stops there for a load of little kids.) Anyway, she just said, "Murky's jerky," which is what she always says.

MURKY'S
PIKPOK
SISTER
↓

It was kind of like when Dwight was trying to be normal at his other school to fit in. But Murky didn't have any reason to act normal at our school. Nobody acts normal at our school.

So anyway, this went on for a few days, and then one day we were at lunch. And Sara and Amy were sitting at the next table with Rhondella, who refuses to ever sit with us.

So then Tater Tot came over to talk to Sara. And at first we were just eavesdropping, but we all ended up being in on the conversation, which went like this:

Sara: Hey, Tater Tot. How's your part of the Rebel
          Alliance? Still hanging in there?

THE TOT
←

OK, I ADMIT I HAVE
NO IDEA HOW TO DRAW
A VOLLEYBALL

Tater Tot: Oh, yeah, I forgot to tell you. I got the girls' volleyball team to join. That's seven eighth graders and four seventh graders that I don't think we had before.

Amy: Excellent news! I'll add them to our totals . . .

Tater Tot: Yeah . . . great! But, uh, I also have some not-great news. Guys, I need to tell you what I just heard. You know that sixth grader, Murky?

Kellen: Yeah, he's one of my best friends.

Tater Tot: Well, these other sixth graders totally crapped all over him, and I heard them bragging about it in the gym.

ME

Lance: What did they do?

Tater Tot: Well, first, do you know if he is . . . uh . . . you know . . .

Lance: What? Middle Eastern? Yeah, his parents are from Turkey.

Tater Tot: DUH! I know that. Everybody knows that. I mean . . . is he . . . gay?

Lance and Kellen and Tommy and Sara: WHAT?

Tater Tot: Well, you know, he is sort of . . . gaylike. Look, don't get mad. I was just asking . . . because

TURKEY

that's what all those other sixth graders think.
That he's gay.

Mike: Stop saying that. It's a bad word! You're going to get us in trouble!

Sara: "Gay" isn't a bad word. It's only bad if you use it as an insult. My uncle is gay and he says it MIKE all the time.

Tater Tot: Well...I guess...but listen, these sixth graders ARE using it as an insult.

Lance: Have they been picking on Murky? Is that why he's all weird lately?

Tater Tot: Worse than just picking on him . . . See, remember Monday was picture day, right? And after we all got our yearbook photos LANCE taken, they did big photos of the whole grade, right? Where we all stood together and the guy was on top of the bleachers?

Rhondella: Right. I helped the photographer with all of that. He—

Tater Tot: Yeah, well . . . Do you remember what Murky wore that day? Probably not, but apparently it was a pink shirt. A really bright pink shirt.

And one of those sixth graders was like, "Oh, great, who gets to stand next to the pink gay guy when they take our photo?"

And the rest were all like, "Not me," and then they got the idea to trick Murky. So after lunch one of them told him everybody was supposed to go back to their homeroom class for the picture, when really everybody was supposed to go straight to the gym.

So apparently he went and sat around in an empty room by himself for ten minutes, and by the time he got to the gym the sixth-grade photo had already been taken and everybody was walking back to class.

And so he asked the guy who lied to him why he lied to him, and the guy goes, "Maybe next time you won't wear the world's gayest shirt on picture day."

Harvey:	How do YOU know all this?
Tater Tot:	Dude, because those guys have been laughing about it all week!
Kellen:	Who?
Tater Tot:	You know . . . Craig and Kurt and those guys.
Kellen:	Your fan base!

CRAIG

kURT

Tater Tot: Don't blame me! I told them they were being butts, but they just think it was okay because he's gay.

Lance: Are they just saying it like "he's so gay," or do they really think he's gay?

Tater Tot: I think they really think he is ... and, I mean, is he?

Sara: What does that have to do with anything?

Tater Tot: I—

Sara: The whole point of those pictures is that everybody is supposed to be in them.

SARA

Rhondella: Yeah, that dork Craig isn't in charge of who gets to be in the yearbook!

Tater Tot: Why are you yelling at me? I didn't do it! I wasn't even there! We did the seventh-grade pictures BEFORE lunch, remember? I'm trying to help him out!

Harvey: Isn't it too late for that?

Tater Tot: I don't know. I just figured you guys should know. We're all on the same team now, right? We're the rebels!

HARVEY

Lance: You're right. Thanks, man.

[And then everybody thanked Tater Tot, and the girls hugged him ... even Sara. Tommy was pretending he

49

wasn't watching that, but his eyes were popping out like Jar Jar's! Then Tater Tot left and we started talking about what to do.]

Lance: I'd like to clobber those jerks.

Harvey: Aside from the fact that they would clobber you...

Lance: Not all of us. Not if we all went after them together.

Harvey: No, they would still clobber all of us. Have you seen those guys? They look—and smell—like Gamorrean guards!

Sara: And anyway, that wouldn't change things for Murky. Do you think they could retake the photo, Rhondella?

Rhondella: No, the photographer comes that day and then comes back the next day to get headshots of kids who were absent the first day, and then that's it. He's already e-mailed the photos to Mrs. Doughty.

Lance: Why Mrs. Doughty?

Rhondella: DUH! She was the yearbook teacher when

it was an elective and now she's still in charge, and we go to her room after school on Wednesdays to work on it. I don't know how we're supposed to get it all done when—

Kellen: Wait! The photos are on her computer in her room, right? You could go in there and use her computer to photoshop Murky back in the picture.

Rhondella: Uh ... do you know how much trouble I would get in for something like that? Mrs. Doughty is nice, but she is a little bit crazy about the yearbook. You DON'T mess with her computer.

[All this time Dwight had been just sitting there picking at his HunnyHam and remembering the good old days of Rib-B-Qs. I didn't even know he'd been listening, but all of a sudden he was holding out Origami Yoda.]

Origami Yoda: Mess with it you must.

Rhondella: Um ... no. I said I wasn't doing the puppet thing. Plus, I'm sorry, but I'm not going to get kicked off of the yearbook for Murky's pink shirt.

Origami Yoda: Must!

Rhondella: Pack it up, Dwight. Yoda's not going to talk me into doing something that stupid.

Dwight: I'm not even—

Origami Yoda: Enough, Dwight! Serious this is! Give her Ahsoka . . .

[Dwight pulled out his backpack and started digging around in it.]

Rhondella: No, I don't need a puppet!

Sara: Yes, you do . . .

Amy: Yeah.

Dwight: Here she is. Be careful with her. The creases on the montrals keep coming uncreased.

[Rhondella looked at it like it was the cheese from Wimpy Kid.]

Rhondella: I said NO PUPPETS!

Dwight: She's actually not a puppet. She's a USB drive holder.

[He pulled a little USB drive out of her head.]

Lance: Excellent! Rhondella, all you'd have to do is slip in there, plug in the USB drive, and get the file for us. It will take ten seconds. We'll do the photoshopping at home.

Kellen: Please?

Harvey: I know Murky irritates you as much as he does
             me, but he is a good guy.

Sara: Just think how you're going to feel if the
             yearbook comes out without Murky and you
             know those jerks won.

Rhondella: Okay, okay, give me the drive, but keep the . . .
             whatever.

Kellen: It's Ahsoka Tano from *The Clone Wars*. She's
             perfect for a stealth mission like this!

Sara: Just think of it as a good-luck charm!

Rhondella: It's a piece of folded-up paper. Now, do you
             want me to do this or not?

Lance: Yes!

Rhondella: All right . . . Mrs. Doughty is right over there
             on lunch duty. So I should be able to do it right
             now. I'll be back.

    Sara and Amy offered to go with her, but she said that
would just seem suspicious. She just walked up to Mrs.
Doughty and asked to go to the bathroom. Then she left.
Then she came back. Then she gave us the USB drive.

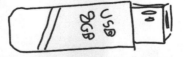

"There it is," she said. "See? I didn't need the puppet."

Then I (Kellen) went over to Murky's after school and took a picture of him with my brother's phone. I told him it was for an art project and that his pink shirt would look good for it. Then we (me and Lance) stuck him in the front row of the class photo using my dad's computer.

And then we gave Craig and Kurt pink shirts, too.

And then we saved it back to the USB drive. The next day we gave that to Rhondella, and she used the same bathroom excuse again to leave the cafeteria.

Then a minute later we saw Mrs. Doughty get up and leave the cafeteria, too.

"Whut the Hutt?" I (Kellen) said. "Mrs. Doughty's headed back to her room!"

WUG! "WUG!" groaned Sara as she jumped out of her seat. She ran over and tried to stall Mrs. Doughty, but it didn't work, because Mr. Howell, who had taken over lunchroom duty, wouldn't let her leave.

Mrs. Doughty went back to her classroom and found Rhondella messing with the yearbook computer. And freaked.

But Rhondella says she had replaced the picture before she got caught, and she told Mrs. Doughty she was just going to check her PhotoWallrus site for new comments. Mrs. Doughty was still mad, and Rhondella got in a lot of trouble but didn't get kicked off the yearbook.

Lastly, we e-mailed a copy of the picture to Murky. We didn't say anything about all the gay stuff, we just sent him the picture and told him to zoom in.

And he said, "Stooky!"

Harvey's Comment

Rhondella really should have used Ahsoka. origami Anakin says, "Nobody does a stealth mission like my Padawan!"

My Comment: Is it just me or is Harvey starting to sound more like Dwight than Dwight?

I have to admit, I do wonder if Murky really is gay. I mean, he's not what I thought gay guys were supposed to be like, but then again I don't know any gay guys. Or at least I don't know that I know any gay guys.

Kellen's Comment

ALL I KNOW IS MURKY = STOOKY!

STOOKY!

HARVEY + ANAKIN

ORIGAMI ANAKIN: EPISODE 1— A PADAWAN'S PLAN

CHANGING PEOPLE FOR THE BETTER—EVEN HARVEY.
BY HARVEY

I'm going to say something that is going to freak you people out:

origami Yoda was right.

I'll give you a minute to freak out. When you've calmed down again, I'll tell you more.

Ready?

I'm not saying I believe that that green paperwad is "real" or that Dwight is some kind of genius. All I'm saying is, in this case, applying the wisdom of Yoda makes sense. Logical sense. And I admit I wouldn't have thought of it without Dwight's help.

okay, remember that thing about Mr. Tolen, the

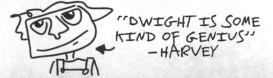

"DWIGHT IS SOME KIND OF GENIUS"
—HARVEY

world's worst PE teacher, and the sit-ups?

He and I had been arguing all year about which kind was better, bent leg or straight leg. But then origami Yoda told me that it doesn't really matter which kind is better. Doing the sit-ups isn't all about developing abdominal muscles, and PE isn't all about getting exercise.

Origami Yoda told me I needed to learn patience and discipline. Just like Anakin, I needed to be a Padawan before I could be a Jedi Knight.

So I started doing the sit-ups Tolen's way. And the basketball drills. And all of Tolen's other Jedi Trials and Tests of Spirit.

But I also started thinking about what all that patience and discipline should lead to. I mean, what's the point if I don't actually get a chance to be a Jedi Knight?

I certainly wasn't a Jedi Knight when we actually played basketball in PE. It's hard to be a Jedi Knight when (a) no one ever passes you the ball and (b) if you do get it, Tater Tot or one of his Totty minions basically attacks you to get it back.

Then the weather warmed up and we went outside

COACH

HARVEY
CUNNINGHAM
JEDI
KNIGHT!

A
SCIENTIFIC
COMPARISON

AT LAST! SOMEONE UNDERSTANDS!

for baseball. And basically the same thing happened all over again. I don't cry like Mike but I will admit that I understand his thing about angry tears.

There's nothing worse than waiting and waiting for your chance to unleash the force on the other team and then someone hits the ball over your head and you run and run and run and everybody is yelling at you and you know you'll be half an hour too late and you are. And then Mr. Tolen says, "Gotta use your head, Harvey," as if he is smarter than you instead of the other way around times fifty. ARRRRGGHH!

And the Dark Side is so inviting right then. All you need to do is step into it and you know you could destroy the feeble-brained Mr. Tolen with one sentence. Maybe two. Delivered at the top of your lungs so everyone in the school can hear.

"Patience, Padawan. Discipline you must learn."

Origami Yoda's words stopped me over and over again. But Origami Anakin and I do not have infinite patience. We were ready to put all that practice to work. Ready to beat Tolen by beating Tater Tot! Ready to finally win something!

But how? All this FunTime stuff didn't matter to Tolen. He wouldn't care if we stopped it or not, so the Rebellion wouldn't hurt him. I had to beat him at his own game.

And then it rained.

You remember that big rain? And we had to have PE inside for a week?

We did a bunch of pointless indoor baseball drills, and one day we played a trivia game. At first I assumed I would win, but then I realized all the questions were about sports. That ended badly.

And then on the last day, because everyone was sick of the drills and stuff, we played crab soccer with one of those huge balls from the equipment closet.

Everybody—even Tater Tot—was out there scooting around on their behinds, because it's hard to walk like a crab. Sometimes someone scuttled a little ways, but mostly people just waited for the big ball to come near them. Then they kicked at it. It's hard to kick accurately from the crab position, so the whole thing was totally random. After thirty minutes of kicking, yelling, and butt sliding, the score was 1–2.

KELLEN'S GUIDE TO CRAB SOCCER...

NOOOOO!

YOU

GIANT BALL

COMING SOON: SPLAT!

59

It had taken most of that time just to get used to crab walking.

"To win, one must be strong when an opponent is weak," I could ALMOST hear origami Anakin say. (But not really. I'm not crazy like some people.)

And then I knew what to do. I knew how to beat Tater Tot. I knew how to show Tolen he had underestimated me.

I knew . . . how to win PE!

It would take patience and discipline and . . . teamwork.

I did need a team. I looked around . . . Mike! He would do anything to win at something. I knew he'd be in.

Lance . . . probably. Amy . . . maybe. Cassie . . . no, she's not exactly one of us.

Dwight . . . ? I looked over at him. Lying on his back in the middle of the gym, trying to spit and then catch it back in his mouth. No . . . too risky.

Then there were kids like Kaleb and Jeffrey. They didn't like me, but they'd been trying to beat Tater Tot all year.

Everyone I asked agreed. I don't expect them to

have as much patience and discipline as I'm going to have. But I know we all want this.

Now we practice . . . a minimum of ten minutes a day of solo crab walking at home. (I do twenty!) And team-practice every chance we get.

Now we plan . . . strategy sessions at lunch and whenever we're in PE sitting on the bench watching Tater Tot hit home runs.

Now we wait . . . for rain.

And when it does, we will join together and RULE THE GALAXY!

My Comment: Or actually . . . RULE ONE HALF OF THE GYM!

CASSIE AS "OLIVIA"

ORIGAMI YODA AND "OLIVIA TWIST," PART 2

BY CASSIE

Wow, just wow! It was amazing!

Okay . . . let me back up.

Remember how our play, *Olivia Twist*, was just suddenly not going to happen because chorus class was canceled for FunTime and the chorus teacher was the drama coach and she basically got fired, I guess?

And then Dwight and Origami Yoda told me that we should put on the play, anyway? And Lunchman Jeff would help us, since the stage is in the cafeteria and he has the key to the backstage area?

And then we were going to rehearse it in Miss Bauer's room before school?

Rehearsals went well even though they were in a classroom and not on the actual stage.

We realized that we wouldn't be able to do the whole play, since lunch is only thirty-five minutes and we'd need to give people ten minutes to sit down and another five minutes to yak a bit.

OH GOODY! AM I IN THIS PLAY?

So we cut out the two corniest musical numbers and a bunch of scenes. We got it down to three songs in twenty minutes. (Frankly, I think the play is much better this way, because it did get kind of boring in the middle before.)

Harvey refused to let us cut his song, of course, but it's actually kind of a fun one because all the orphans dance and wave spoons at him while he sings.

Sara is actually much better than Brianna was, and her part is small, so she learned it pretty quick.

After a month of meeting before school, we were ready for the real thing.

So this morning, instead of practicing, we carried all our props (we didn't have any scenery) to the stage. Lunchman Jeff had already unlocked the door for us. We snuck everything in and set it up without getting caught.

PROPS:

SPOONS +BOWLS • ULGY HATS • OLD RAGGY SUITS • JAZZ HANDS

I was worried about Rabbski seeing us, but she wasn't around.

But I knew she probably would be around during lunch, so I asked Dwight and Origami Yoda what to do about it.

"Leave it to me, m'lady. I have a plan," Dwight said in his Sherlock Dwight voice.

"Uh, what's your plan? Can you definitely keep her out of the cafeteria for the whole lunch period or not?" I asked.

But of course I should have known he wouldn't actually tell me.

"I would think that the plan might be obvious to you at this point," said Sherlock Dwight. "It really is quite elem—"

"Don't say it! Just do it!" I said.

So it looked like we were all set for opening night, which was really opening lunch.

The first scene is the big orphanage scene. Everybody—even people who had other parts later— was dressed like an orphan and holding an empty bowl and a wooden spoon. And I was supposed to say to Harvey, who was the evil orphanage director, "Please,

sir, I want some more," and then we start the big musical number, "We Want More."

So we all got in place, and Tommy, who volunteered to be the stage manager, opened the curtains and . . .

YAY! I AM IN THE PLAY!

Nobody noticed. Everybody just kept eating and yakking, just like Harvey had told us a million times that they would. Some people did look at the stage, but when I said my line, they obviously couldn't hear me.

It was a total disaster!

I tried to glare at Dwight, but HE WASN'T EVEN LOOKING!

And then I saw one person who was looking: Ms. Rabbski! Sherlock Dwight totally did nothing! Then I saw her start running for the stage door.

Great! We were going to get busted after performing ONE SENTENCE of our play!

The curtains started closing.

I looked backstage, which was actually just a tiny room to the side of the stage, and Tommy was there pulling on the curtain rope and he pointed to the back and Ms. Rabbski was over there unlocking a little cabinet.

I was bracing for her to call our whole play a

"disruption to the learning environment" and send us all to ISS, or worse.

But that's not what happened!

"Why didn't you tell me?" she hollered. "We've got a couple of wireless mics and three regular ones . . .

Nobody could understand what was going on. Why wasn't she exploding at us?

"Well, quickly now! Cassie and Harvey better have the wireless mics, for this scene at least. Now, let me see if I can get this PA system turned on. Mr. Good Clean Fun uses it more than I do . . ."

Suddenly there was an insane screeching noise.

"Ah, well, that's it," said Rabbski. "You should be good to go. Places! Tommy, hit that curtain!

The curtain went back up. EVERYBODY was looking to find out why their eardrums had just exploded.

I was still clipping on the microphone, and I was holding my empty bowl in one hand and the battery pack in the other. I turned to Harvey.

"PLEASE, SIR, I WANT SOME MORE!"

I wasn't shouting; the mic was just that loud.

"More?" bellowed Harvey. I think Rabbski had turned the volume down, but Harvey was really shouting. I hate to say this, but he was incredible. He really looked like he was enraged because I wanted more gruel.

"YOU WANT MORE, YOU MISERABLE ORPHAN? YOU'VE HAD ALL YOU'RE GOING TO GET, BY GEORGE!"

The music started! I glanced over. Tommy was holding the CD player and Rabbski was actually holding one of the microphones in front of it.

We did the song, the dance, the whole play . . . or at least the whole twenty-minute version of the whole play.

The bell rang right when I was getting adopted by Lance and Sara, so we sort of got a standing ovation because everybody had to stand up to go to class, but some people did actually clap while they were lining up.

Most importantly, the whole thing was a blast and I finally got to be the star and Rabbski wasn't mad at anybody. In fact she said we "had spunk," which apparently is a good thing.

* NOT A MURKYISM, BELIVE I

YOU'VE GOT SPUNK! *

Thank you, thank you ... No autographs, please ...

My Comment: I am so sorry I doubted Origami Yoda. I was mad when he started this whole play thing, because Sara wouldn't be in the library in the morning. Then Sara asked if I wanted to be the stage manager, so . . .

COURSE OF!

we ended up hanging out together maybe even more than usual! So Origami Yoda was looking out for me after all! And apparently Sherlock Dwight had it all figured out the whole time.

But there was one thing I couldn't figure out. How could he have known that Ms. Rabbski would be so HAPPY we were putting on the play? I can see how Origami Yoda might have predicted that—but how could Sherlock Dwight have "logically" figured it out?

So I asked Dwight.

"Elementary, my dear Tommy!" he said. "The answer is—as most answers are—in the library! Reference shelf two, yearbook section, 1981 edition, page seventy-five."

So I went and looked it up. The yearbook was called Personalities '81 back then. Page seventy-five was for the drama club. The star of two of the three plays that

Personalities '81

year was a girl with really shiny hair named . . . Lulu
Rabbski.

I looked through the rest of the book and found that
Lulu was runner-up in the spelling bee, was a member
of the chess club, and dressed up as a robot from the
old-timey version of *Battlestar Galactica* for Halloween.

I showed the picture to Kellen, and he said, "She's
cute!" Then I showed him the name, and he said,
"BLEEARGHHHHHH!"

LULU RABBSKI!!!!!

DWIGHT + YODA

YOU CAN SKIP THIS ONE.

DWIGHT GETS WEIRD(ER)

BY TOMMY

There is one new problem the Rebellion is facing: Dwight is getting REALLY weird.

Yes, yes, I know it's weird that until recently he wore a cape and called himself Captain Dwight, but now he says he isn't even part of the Rebellion, but Origami Yoda still is.

That's just base-level Dwight weirdness. People would probably be okay with that.

Now Dwight is doing some new weird stuff that kind of reminds you of the days before

Origami Yoda. So here's a new Top 10.

GIVE IT UP AlREADY!

10. You know that jokey sort of thing where you tell someone they can't kiss their elbow and then they try for thirty seconds and give up? Well, Dwight has been trying for three weeks.

9. You know that book report Kellen failed? Well, Dwight got an A+ for writing a seventeen-page report called "From Stuart Little to Babymouse: A Comparison and Evaluation of Talking Rodentia in Children's Literature." And, no, it wasn't copied off the Internet.

I LIKE TALKING RODENTS. *

SQUIRRELNUTKIN

8. This may have been going on for a long time and maybe I just noticed it . . . but he never says anyone's name when he's talking to them. Does he know our names? I don't know!

* I LIKE NUTS!

7. He must have gotten a bag of that plastic Easter-basket grass, because one day he showed up with it taped to his face like a beard.

6. Then he missed a day of school because some of the plastic grass "somehow" got stuck up inside his nose and he had to go to a doctor to get it out.

5. Sara says that that big rain filled up the holes in Dwight's backyard—but he sat in them, anyway! (Which at least explains the big brown stains on his overalls!)

4 He's been trying to fold a new piece of origami. But he can't seem to get it right. He'll be totally quiet for ten minutes, and then all of a sudden you'll just hear him yell, "Bantha dung!" and then he crumples

it up. From what we can tell by examining the crumples, it appears to be a new puppet. Some sort of bat? Anyway, it would be best if he would stop with the yelling, especially IN THE MIDDLE OF SOCIAL STUDIES!

JARJAR?
BATMAN?
JARMAN?

3. He has a fake thumb. I don't mean one of his thumbs on his hands is fake. Those are both real—as far as I know!—but sometimes you'll notice that he's wearing a fake plastic thumb over one of the real thumbs. If you ask him about it, he will wave the other hand around in the air while he tries to slip the plastic thumb into his pocket.

2. One day at lunch he wouldn't eat. He would pick up his fork, then put it down, and then rub his fingers. After this happened a thousand times, Amy said, "Is there

HI, JARMAN!

HI, WILLY THE WALKING WAFFLE!

BEETS

DWIGHT'S FORK → ⊐ 2.1MM

NORMAL FORK → ⊐ 2.2MM

something wrong with your fork?"

"I'm not comfortable with the thickness of the handle."

"Do you want to trade? I haven't used mine."

They traded and he ate his lunch.

I checked the "bad" fork, and it was just a normal fork.

1.   These e-mails with Caroline:

Can you possibly explain what this noise/song is that Dwight keeps mumbling / grunting / singing?

Reading his lips, it seems like he is saying, "Ah Pa Fa Ta Sta" over and over again—and I mean a lot of times. Through a whole meal at Wendy's.

When I ask him what he's singing, he stops for a few minutes, but he won't tell me.

You know I hate to ask people to repeat themselves, but when I do and then they refuse, that makes me mad.

When we have our non-dates at Wendy's, my dad

sits at another table until it's time to go. But this time, I had him come over while we ate our Frosties, because I was hoping he'd be able to tell me what Dwight was sing-mumbling.

When we got in the car to go, I asked him what it sounded like.

"As best as I can tell," he said, "it was 'Ah Pa Fa Ta Sta.' That is some boyfriend you got."

(Dad knows I hate the word "boyfriend.")

So is Dwight doing this at school, and if so, please, please tell me what it is before Dwight drives me crazy!!!

—Caroline

CAROLINE'S
WEIRD
DAD

Caroline—

Does he do it at school? Only ALL DAY, EVERY DAY! He can't stop!

It's from that awful video we have to watch called FunTime. I assume Dwight has told you about it?

Anyway, it's like that song from a few

AT LAST! THE REAL REASON FOR LOBOT'S HEAD PHONES!

STAAH PA FA TA TA FAPA

75

years ago where the guy kept going, "Oppa Gangnam Style," except it's "Oppa FunTime Style."

What I really hate is the way Dwight is apparently playing the rest of the song in his head and just singing that part. It makes it sound like this:

"Oppa FunTime Style. [Pause] Oppa FunTime Style. [Short pause] Oppa FunTime Style. [Long pause]."

And each time he pauses, you think, 'Thank Jabba—maybe that was the last time," but you have to wait to be sure. And the pause goes on and on, and you think, "Okay, it's definitely over," and then, "Oppa FunTime Style!"

Harvey's Comment

Caroline, you have my permission to dump your Frosty over Dwight's head when he does this.

My Comment: Part of the weird thing is that I'm sure Dwight hates the song as much as we do and I think his own mumbling is driving him crazy.

These ten things—and remember these are just the top ten!—are a problem because we are all putting a lot of faith in Origami Yoda and his Rebellion plan. And it's a little weird to take advice from a finger puppet when the guy who owns the finger is trying to kiss his elbow all the time while wearing a green plastic beard and singing a song from the same program that you're taking his advice about how to get rid of!

JUDGE ME BY THIS GUY DO YOU?

AH PA FATAPAH PATAS

AH LATASAH PATA FA SAH PATATAS

PROFESSOR F. + TEVON

2PROFESSORFUNTIME

BY LANCE

I don't really see why I have to type this all up since I just told all of you guys . . . But here goes.

I'M EVEN WORSE ON BLU-RAY.

I finally talked my parents into letting me watch *Parasite Within: Legend of Vampyre* on DVD. I just couldn't believe it was as bad as you guys said it was.

It was. But here's the thing: The very first victim looked totally familiar. The whole rest of the movie I was thinking, who was that guy?

Then later when I was using the bathroom, I realized who it was: PROFESSOR FUNTIME!!!!

I looked up *Parasite Within* on IMDb and found the

VICTIM #1 →

OW... SOMETHING BIT MY TOE ... FROM THE INSIDE!!!

actor. His name is Tevon Riley and he's been in a million lousy movies and TV shows.

Then I went to his Web site. It said "Follow me on Twitter: @TheRealTevon."

So I did, and then I tweeted:

> @TheRealTevon are you also the REAL Professor FunTime?

He wrote back:

> LOL! R they still making u kids watch that ****? SORRY! But don't blame me! Worst. Role. Script. Effects. Songs. Everything. EVER! #HateGizmo.

So even Professor FunTime thinks FunTime is stupid!!!!!!!!!

Harvey's Comment

Wow, when Victim #1 in Legend of Vampyre thinks something is stupid, it must be REALLY, REALLY stupid!

My Comment: Excellent job, Lance! This could be very useful information!

VICTIM #2 WAS ANYONE WHO ACTUALLY WATCHED THE MOVIE!

79

AMY AND R2 CONFRONT RABBSKI, PART 2

BY AMY

"Okay, people, it's been another week!" I said. "And there's Rabbski. I'm going in! I'm going to ask her what she's doing about FunTime."

Harvey said, "Man, you sound a lot more like Luke than Kellen does. Maybe you guys should switch."

"No thanks," I said. "In case you never noticed, it's R2-D2 who actually gets things done in the movies. And did you see that episode of *The Clone Wars* where he leads the all-droid spy mission? R2 rocks! No offense, Luke."

BEEP! WHISTLE

"Uh . . . none taken," mumbled Kellen.

"C'mon, Lance," I said.

"Do I have to go again?" he whined. (If he thinks  he's really going to stay my boyfriend, he's going to have to shape up! And, no, I don't care if he reads this, Tommy. I hope he does! Shape up, LanLan!)

So we went to see Rabbski again.

"Yes, Amy," she said as if I had just asked her an hour ago and not a whole week ago! "I've discussed it all with the superintendent, and he's going to discuss it with the school board . . ."

"Discuss?" I asked. "Is that all that's happened in four weeks?"

Lance was tugging at my sleeve. Did he think I was going to go back and sit down?

"Ms. Rabbski," I said, "we are still watching that stupid program and still missing out on actual classes."

"Okay, calm down, Amy," she said. "I'm trying to be patient with you. I need you to be patient with me."

"Patient?!?"

Lance was practically trying to drag me back across the cafeteria to get away. But frankly I didn't care if I got in trouble right then.

"If we're patient much longer, the year will be over!"

"Listen, Amy. FunTime was a very expensive pilot program," she said. "You can't expect the school board to just give up on it before getting the results."

"Expensive?" said Lance. "Do you mean the school actually has to pay for us to watch those dumb videos?" (Finally, a little backbone! Good job, LanLan!)

And, sadly, the answer to that question was YES. And it's a lot of money. I searched the school board's minutes online and I found all these different "expenditures" where they were paying Edu-Fun tons of money for different things.

"This is madness!" said Lance's C-3PO.

"Long sad whistle with a beep," said R2-D2.

Your parents' tax dollars at work! ←

My Comment: If I hear the word "patient" one more time, I'm going to lose it. We've been waiting so long that Foldy-Wan is changing from Ewan McGregor into Alec Guinness!

THE SAGA OF LUCKYYUCKY

JUST SKIP THIS ONE.

BY JAMES SUERVO, JR.

I never wrote one of the case files before so I don't really know how to do it, but here you go:

Place: The library. Not the one at school but the public library.

ADAM

So one day me and Adam Minch were over at the library, playing Deathbourne on the public computers there. Using the public computers is a challenge because you can only play for one hour and some levels of Deathbourne are really, really hard to beat in less than an hour.

DEATHBOURNE™

The advantage to playing at the library is that my mother doesn't let me play Deathbourne at home.

Anyway, we had been trying to beat Trollwing Tower for a couple of weeks and one day we beat it and I was the one who actually shot the Mithril arrow through the TrollWytch's ice heart.

"This must be my lucky computer!" I said.

And Minch said, "Yeah, I guess the boogers on the mouse helped."

And I looked down and there were some sort of disgusting semi-hardened yet moist globules all over the mouse. Not from me but from someone who had used it before me!!!! And I have a bad feeling it was something worse than boogers! I just don't know what that would be.

I could barely bring myself to click the mouse to hit SAVE, and then I ran for the bathroom and scrubbed for ten minutes.

So the next time we went to play Deathbourne, we looked and the stuff was still all over the mouse!

And the next time, too, and that time some lady was using it, and I almost told her about it but decided maybe she would be happier not knowing.

LALALA... EVERYTHING IS JUST SO PERFECT.

But I was like, why isn't the library cleaning that stuff off?

So as the weeks went by and the globules just stayed there, we named the mouse LuckyYucky. And we started a fan club for it—although I have to admit there were only two of us in the club—and we made T-shirts.

Sometimes we even went in to check on it when we didn't even have time to play Deathbourne. Just to see if anyone had cleaned it off. THEY NEVER DID! I still can't believe it.

Then one day, when we went in to play Death-bourne 2: Realm of the FyreWolves (we had finished Deathbourne 1 by then), there were only two open computers, and one of them had LuckyYucky.

"Good luck with that," said Minch, and he quickly sat down at the other computer.

What was I going to do?

And then I thought about you guys and all your *Star Wars* stuff and I thought about Origami Yoda and realized his advice might be "Clean mouse from home you should bring." Which is a really smart idea. And since then I HAVE been doing that.

But right at that moment I needed to do something! Then I remembered Hando Calrissian, and even though he had rubbed all the way off, I thought about what he would have done. He would have cleaned it off himself.

So I did.

And that was the end of LuckyYucky . . .

Not quite a happy ending, because we got totally hammered by the fyrewolves that day. LuckyYucky wasn't lucky once he lost the yucky.

Harvey's Comment

Sometimes I think this whole origami Yoda thing just boils down to "clues for the clueless." Also, Deathbourne is a total rip-off of CorpseWrath: Midnight Dark.

My Comment: I think I'll follow Origami Yoda's advice. I mean, just because you don't SEE something gross on a library mouse doesn't mean the last person didn't wipe something gross yet invisible on it.

IS IT HOT IN HERE OR IS IT JUST ME?

SOAPY

THE @&$#! FATE OF SOAPY THE MONKEY

BY QUAVONDO

Tommy, don't let just anyone read this, okay?

If this falls into the wrong hands—my sister's—it would be a big mess.

Because I have to tell you about what I saw at Derwin's BBQ #2.

QUAVONDO'S SISTER

But to do that I have to explain why I was at Derwin's BBQ #2 and not #1 and also why I was at a BBQ restaurant at all when I'm a vegetarian.

But I'll try to keep that short so I can get to the point . . .

1.   My brother, Thanh, was home from college for spring break.

QUAVONDO'S BROTHER

2. I told him my secret about not really being a vegetarian, but how the Fortune Wookiee told me to be one and it saved me from Grandma's infamous meat loaf, the Big Pink.

3. My brother said the Fortune Wookiee's plan is brilliant and he might try it, too, if Grandma fixes the Big Pink for Easter.

4. I begged him to drive me somewhere for a big MEATY meal.

5. He suggested the Chinese Buffet on Williamson Road, but I told him about what happened when we took Grandma there last time she came to town:

CRAB RANGOON! MMMMM...

   A. We had a nice meal.

   B. When we were leaving, a lady customer was walking in. The lady looked at us and said, "Well, if you all eat here, this place must be pretty good."

   C. Grandma said, "What do you mean?" But I think she already knew what the lady meant.

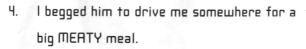

   D. My mom tried to push my grandma out the door before she could start a

cuss-word-filled lecture at the lady about the difference between Vietnam and China. And how it was none of her *&^@# business where we ate. She was too late. EVERYBODY heard.

E.   We've all been too embarrassed to go back there again, even without Grandma.

6.   So then Thanh said he could go for some Derwin's BBQ.

7.   I said I could, too, but could we go to Derwin's #2, since we might see someone I knew at Derwin's #1.

8.   So that's why we ended up at Derwin's #2 all the way across town. (It's just as good as #1 and there's plenty of tables so you don't have to eat standing up like at Derwin's #1, AND there's a buffet.)

So . . . we got the buffet and we kept going back over and over and over. We had a huge pile of dirty plates on our table.

A busboy pushed a cart over to clear away some of the dirty dishes. I noticed he was wearing enormous rubber gloves that went all the way up to his elbows.

And then I recognized him.

"I know you! You're Mr. Good Clean Fun!" I said.

He looked at me and said, "And I know you. You're the Cheeto Hog of McQuarrie Middle School!"

"Uh, they don't call me that anymore," I said.

"Well, they don't call me Mr. Good Clean Fun anymore, either," he said.

"Nobody calls me Thanh at college," said my brother. "So we're, like, three nameless dudes!"

"Uh . . . I do have a real name," said Mr. GCF. "It's Adam."

"What are you doing here?" I asked.

"Oh, well, times are tight for all of us school assembly performers. Schools don't want my old hygiene act anymore. The money is in test pep rallies. I've been trying to put together a new act for that, but . . . er, I guess you saw what happened."

"Yeah," I said. The entire event had been a disaster, starting with bad fake pizza and ending with kids mocking his songs. "Sorry about that."

DON'T BLAME ME!

"Ah, don't worry about it. Frankly, I'd rather keep working here than sell out like that anyhow. Listen, I better take these dishes back."

"Wait," I said. "Where's Soapy?"

"He's out in my van with the rest of the show stuff," said Adam, with kind of a sarcastic laugh. "I'll tell him you said hi."

He started to push his cart away, then came back to our table.

"Here are some moist towelettes. It's always best to sanitize your hands before and after visiting the buffet line."

Guys, I feel awful for him. It's sort of our fault that he's given up! We broke his spirit!

Kit Fisto thinks we can save him, though.

"We're already trying to do the impossible," Kit told me. "This part should be easy."

I think we need to add Mr. Good Clean Fun to our list of demands. We'll tell Rabbski we want a REAL Good Clean Fun assembly, not a test pep rally!

Harvey's Comment

Great idea! There's just one tiny problem ... we DON'T want a Good Clean Fun assembly, real or otherwise!

oh, and don't worry about me telling anyone about you going to Derwin's . . . I'd be afraid of boring them to death!

My Comment: Wow, Harvey, sometimes you make Boba Fett seem like a nice, sympathetic guy.

But I guess I have to agree. This is like when Dwight wanted to rebel over the Rib-B-Qs. We can't make too many demands. We're already out on a limb by adding JV sports, in my opinion.

So . . . I think we'll just have to wait and see if we can do something later.

HARVEY

ORIGAMI ANAKIN: EPISODE II—CRISIS IN THE CRAB NEBULA

BY HARVEY

At first, it was like living on Tatooine. No rain! At least not during our gym period.

"What if the year ends without us having PE inside again?" asked Mike.

"That would be nostrul," said Amy.

"The odds of not having at least one rainy day during April are ten kabillion to one," said Lance's C-3PO.

And he (Lance, not his crinkly C-3 Paperwad) was right. Finally it did rain. And the extra time had just let us get better and better.

We discovered that once you learn how to crab RUN—not crab walk, but crab RUN!—the game is actually a lot of fun. We played three times in Lance's backyard and it was—I hate to use this word, but what else can I say?—awesome!

Yes, I, Harvey, had fun playing a sport. (The best part, however, was when Mike put his hand in some of Lance's dog's poop. Actually, that was the best part of anything ever!)

Tommy, Quavondo, and Kellen played some, too, even though they have Ms. Toner for gym and she doesn't do crab soccer. When it rains, she lets them use the gymnastics equipment on the other side of the gym partition.

Anyway . . . we played, we practiced, and we got really good. Probably as good as anyone has ever gotten at crab soccer anywhere.

BUT . . . there was one thing I had never thought of: What if we had to play WITH Tater Tot instead of against him?

That's what happened.

When it finally did rain and Tolen had us stay

Tot

in to play crab soccer, he didn't split us into two teams.

He came out of the equipment closet dragging the nets and kicking the big crab soccer ball and said, "Ms. Toner's got a sub today. So we're going to open the partition, and you guys are going to play Ms. Toner's class."

That meant ... we would be on Tater Tot's team! And we would be playing Tommy and Kellen!

Tolen blew the whistle and everybody dropped to their butts. Then he tossed the big ball into the middle of the floor. And people started their usual scooting and scuttling and waiting. Except for us. We started moving ... fast!

The ball had landed near Mike, and he zoomed toward it.

"Lock S-foils in attack position!" he yelled.

That was the code for our best play. Instead of blindly scooting toward the ball like everyone else, me and Kaleb went down the court on the left. Amy and Jeffrey went down the right. And Mike moved toward the goal, just in case anyone got the ball

away from Lance. Fat chance! Lance was flying. He was dribbling the ball down the court ... No one ever dribbles in crab soccer. But we had practiced!

Of course, Tommy and Kellen had practiced, too. Kellen came at Lance from the side.

Amy yelled, "I'm open," and Lance kicked the ball to her. "Get ready, Harvey," she hollered.

Amy popped the ball over some people right to me. It was a perfect shot. I didn't even have to bring it down.

I did a wampa kick. That's one Lance invented where you drop to your back and kick with both legs.

A perfect shot! Right at the goal! And ... Tommy came crab sprinting into the goal and deflected it at the last second! (Tommy, I have to admit, you can move your tiny little body very fast! Anakin/Darth Paper: "Most impressive!")

It wasn't going to be easy to beat Toner's class after all! We set up another shot and Jeffrey blasted it with his patented Starkiller kick. Tommy kicked that one out of bounds, too.

WHOMP!

WAMPA KICK!

It almost clonked Mr. Tolen in the head. He was standing there looking at us like he couldn't believe it.

He blew his whistle and threw the ball back in . . . right to Quavondo, who kicked it really hard to the other end of the gym. It was going to take some hard work to get back into scoring position.

I went near Tater Tot as I raced after the ball.

"Are you guys actually playing for real?" he asked.

"Yes!" I shouted back as I went past him.

"I'm in!" he hollered. And he was! With no practice, he just turned it on and was almost as good as us. ALMOST!

It was a WILD game, but no one was scoring. With Tommy as their goalie and Mike as ours, all shots were getting blocked. And it was hard to get set up for a shot, because so many kids were basically annoying, do-nothing obstacles. (Actually, a lot of them are like that outside of PE, too!)

So, with time running out, the score was still 0—0.

Despite all our practice I was getting exhausted. My hands were killing me. But except for Tater Tot we had left everybody in the dust.

And Mike had had an incredible moment when he totally rejected a shot by this obnoxious guy, Drevin, who used to yell "Easy out" at Mike all the time. Mike blocked the shot right back in his face and Drevin had to go "take a cooldown" on the bleachers! (There's a tip for you, Mike: Never cry in PE—just go "take a cool down.")

THINK I'LL GO TAKE A COOL DOWN...

And then Amy put some kind of crazy spin move on Kellen and started a break for the goal. (Have you ever tried to spin in crab position? Not easy!)

"I'm open!" Tater Tot and I both yelled at the same time. But Tater Tot was closer and she kicked it to him.

I hate to admit it, but his ball-handling skills were excellent for someone who had only been playing for half an hour.

He was headed for Tommy and the goal.

As I crabbed up there to watch, I realized the horror of what was happening. After all our hard work, all we had done was set the stage for another Tater Tot victory.

Tater Tot was going to score, and the only thing

ANOTHER TOT VICTORY . . .

anyone would remember was that the Tot had won again. The nerdy kids who had put forth an effort that day would be mentioned only to add to Tater Tot's glory.

I was just about to yell "Nooooooo!" when Tater Tot faked a kick to the left, totally fooling Tommy, and then brought his leg back to make an amazing backward kick . . . straight to me.

"It's all yours, kid!" he yelled.

one part of my brain was correcting his Han Solo quote—it's "You're all clear, kid"—but the other part drew on all the practice, all the discipline, everything we had learned . . .

I flung myself forward but didn't kick . . . I let the ball bounce right in front of me . . . waited until it was just hanging there . . . and wampa-kicked it right into the goal!

We won!!!! The Padawans had become the Masters!

My Comment: Great. Hooray. Wheeee. Everybody's a winner . . . except me!

No, I'm just kidding! That was just my Harvey

imitation. I can honestly say that was the best PE class ever!

Unfortunately, the sun came out, and the next day we were back to being losers again. No, I don't mean that, either . . . I mean, we still lose. But now we know what we're capable of.

I AM SICK OF DRAWING CRAB SOCCER . . .
SO I'LL US THIS SPACE TO DRAW
WILLY THE WALKING WAFFLE
IN THE **WIZARD OF OZ!**

I'M MELTING! MELTING

WICKED WITCH OF THE BUTTER

THAT'S THE DUMBEST THING I'VE EVER SEEN!

SARA

MAY THE FLUSH BE WITH YOU(?)

BY SARA

So we were sitting there at lunch and I was at the Rebellion table with Tommy and everybody this time since Rhondella was eating at Jen's table.

And this kid I had NEVER seen before in my life comes up and taps me on the shoulder and hands me this packet of folded-up papers. Then he walk/runs away before I can say anything.

"Uh . . . who was that guy?" I asked.

"Oh, that was Cody C.," said Kellen. "You don't know Cody C.?"

"Codeesy?" I asked, confused.

CODY F.
CODY C.

"No, Cody . . . C., like the letter 'C,' because there are two Codys in Patterns, and the other one is Cody F."

"What is 'Patterns'?"

"Geez, don't you know anything?" asked Lance.

And I felt like, no, I don't know anything all of sudden.

"You know," said Kellen, "the Patterns classroom, at the end of B wing?"

"Oh, yeah . . . ," I said. "I didn't know that was called Patterns."

A girl I know from church, Sadie, is in that classroom, and I see her being pushed down the hall sometimes. At church her mother is always hovering over her, and in the hall an aide is always with her. So I have to admit that I've never actually spoken to her. Plus, I'm not exactly sure what to say or if she'd understand me or be able to talk to me.

SADIE

"WELL, open the letter already!" said Amy, practically yanking my arm off. "Maybe it's a LOVE letter!"

So I opened it.

It was five pieces of paper. Each one written and/or drawn by a different person.

The top one was from Cody C. himself. It was a

drawing of toilets. Not a drawing like artwork, more like a blueprint or something.

Underneath that was a perfect drawing of some video game character. [Tommy's note: Sonic the Hedgehog, and yes, it was perfect in every detail!]

And underneath that was a weather map, then a mosaic made from ripped-up FunTime worksheets, and then a drawing of a unicorn.

"These are neat," I said, "but I don't— Oh!"

That's when I noticed that the unicorn's horn had skewered Gizmo the calculator.

"This weather map shows a hurricane about to hit FunTime City!" said Kellen.

"Yeah," said Tommy, "and look at this Sonic drawing. At first I thought that was Dr. Eggman, but it's actually a Dr. Eggman/Professor FunTime mash-up!"

"Agreed," said Harvey. "And notice that the mosaic appears to be an abstract rendering of the Emperor's throne room from *Return of the Jedi*."

He was right! When I looked at it closer, I could see the throne, the Emperor, and those weird guards with

the red robes. And then I was shocked to see Sadie's name at the bottom! I had no idea that she could make stuff like that or that she had ever seen *Star Wars*.

"Everything here," said Tommy, "seems to be anti-FunTime!"

"Yeah," said Kellen. "I totally need that Sonic drawing on a T-shirt!"

"What about the toilets?" I asked.

"Check it out," said Lance. "All the pipes come together down here in the corner, and the sewage is dripping out onto a tiny book with feet . . . which can only be Webster the breakdancing dictionary!"

"Wow! Those guys are hard-core. They must hate FunTime as much as we do!"

And that was how five members of the Patterns class joined the Rebellion!

Harvey's Comment

This is a great case file and a really cool story, Sara ... However, I have to complain about the title that TOMMY gave it.

"May the Flush Be with You"??? Seriously? That is disgraceful!

AGREED!

105

It's fine for toilets and flushes and even Kellen to be a part of these case files. But when you replace the force—the mystical energy source that binds all living things together—with "flush," then you are going too far!!!!

Just because a pun CAN be made does not mean it MUST be made!

You are demeaning *Star Wars*, and I cannot be a part of that!

Unless you change it, I will no longer comment or write case files.

My Comment: All right, all right, you're right. I wasn't really thinking. I'll scratch it out.

Kellen's Comment

NO! LEAVE IT IN THERE. I MEAN, I AGREE WITH HARVEY THAT IT'S STUPID AND DISRESPECTFUL TO STAR WARS . . . BUT IF IT MEANS THAT HARVEY IS GOING TO STOP COMMENTING ON THE CASE FILES, THEN KEEP IT!

MS. RABBSKI?

AMY AND R2 CONFRONT RABBSKI, PART 3

SPRING INTO ACTION.

BY AMY

Okay, so this time when we went up to see Ms. Rabbski, she smiled and said, "Ah, Amy, I thought you'd forgotten me."

"Forgotten?" I said. "The only thing that gets us through FunTime is the hope that today is the day you finally have news for us."

"Well, guess what? Today IS the day."

"Really?" said Lance.

"Yes. Your seventh-period teacher will give you a handout to take home today. You guys spoke your minds and we listened! FunTime will be replaced."

YUB NUB

HOLD THE YUB NUBS A MINUTE!

"Tomorrow?" I asked.

"Well, no," she said. "Next year. As I said, the school board wants to see the results of the FunTime pilot project. Also, our grant requires . . ."

She has more to say, but none of it seemed to change the great news that we wouldn't have FunTime next year and the bad news that we would have it for another month or so.

In seventh period, Mr. Randall handed out this paper ➡️

Dear Students and Parents,

This has been an exciting spring here at McQuarrie Middle School.

In an effort to boost state Standards test scores, we've participated in a pilot project funded by a federal grant through the Lucas County Board of Education and cosponsored by Edu-Fun Educational Products, Inc.

Although we haven't taken the tests yet, one thing has been made clear. Our bright, energetic students have not been enjoying the video portion of the FunTime test-prep system.

So I'm pleased to announce that next year, the pilot project will continue, but with an all-new digital learning system: Xtreme.Fun™, Edu-Fun's new high-tech, fully interactive system.

We wish we could begin using the new system today, but new technology will need to be installed over the summer to prepare our classrooms for this state-of-the-art educational experience!

As principal of McQuarrie it is my hope that this resolves complaints from students and parents and allows us to FOCUS on the FUNdamentals again as we get ready to take the actual tests.

And I would like to remind every student that it is their duty to do their best on the test. Students who think they are being "rebels" by purposefully getting a low score are cheating themselves and the school. If these students continue to be disruptions to the learning environment, they WILL face disciplinary action.

Let's stay positive and focused and ACE THOSE TESTS! I truly believe McQuarrie is the best school in the county, and I want those test scores to prove it!

Sincerely,

Lougene Rabbski
Principal
McQuarrie Middle School

"We're doomed," whispered Lance/C-3PO.

"Whirrrrrrr," responded R2-D2 sadly.

Then we heard a distant "NOOOOOO!!" coming from another classroom. Either Harvey or Kellen, I bet.

"My thoughts exactly," said Mr. Randall. And he flopped down in his chair and just sat there.

He looked so depressed that after the bell rang, me and Lance went up to talk to him.

"You guys are lucky. You'll only have one more year of FunTime, and then you'll go to the high school. And I'll be left here with the Professor and his deranged singing calculator on some kind of 3-D jumbo screen."

"Don't worry," I told him. "It's not over yet. The Origami Rebellion isn't giving up!"

"We aren't?" said Lance, or maybe it was C-3PO. I'm not sure. Either way, it was wussy.

"BEEP!" growled R2.

Harvey's Comment

⟶ Yes, that was me shouting, "Noooo!"

My Comment: And it was me and Foldy-Wan saying, "I've got a bad feeling about this."

MIKE + MACE

WHAT NOW?

BY MIKE, THE HOLOCRON KEEPER

Rabbski was smart to give that paper out at the end of the day.

We only had a few seconds to talk about it in the hall before some people had to line up for their buses. I didn't have the recorder, so this is from memory. (You'll notice that I was listening and remembering instead of freaking out. Thanks, Mace!)

Kellen/Luke: We waited a month for that? Anakin was right! All we were doing was letting her set a trap for us.

Harvey/Anakin: We have been totally out-maneuvered by Rabbski. By pretending to let us win, she has us fully in her grip!

Tommy/Foldy-Wan: Now she will begin slowly crushing us to death.

Lance/C-3PO: I am totally sick of this narnar.

Sara/Han Foldo: Basically, she ignored us.

Amy/R2: We need to do something big.

Remi/Mara Jade: I'm ready to go Dark Side. I say we steal all the FunTime DVDs and—

Me (Mike/Mace): HZZZTTT![waving arms] It's Rabbski!

Rabbski: Well, hello everyone! Victory party?

Amy: Victory? For you, maybe. Not for us.

Rabbski: Oh, Amy . . . I've been trying to explain. This isn't a me-versus-you-guys thing. We're all on the same side. Haven't I proven that by listening to you and going to the school board to make this better?

Harvey: Better? What's going to be better about

FunTime: The Next Generation? It's still going to suck.

Rabbski: First, we do NOT use that word at McQuarrie. Second, you haven't even seen it yet. Aren't you willing to give it a chance? You're going to throw this big stink about something you don't know anything about?

[Long silence broken by the Wave 1 bus bell.]

Rabbski: I don't know what to tell you, then. I—I'm surprised. Go get to your buses. Don't let me keep you . . . But I hope you come back tomorrow without the bad attitudes.

We came back the next day. And so did our bad attitudes.

When we met in the library before school, we had a long talk/argument about it. Seriously, there's no way I can type up the whole thing. So I've listened to the recording a couple of times, and these are the major points:

Eighty-seven percent loss of parental support for Rebellion: Most of our parents seem to have said something like, "You're lucky that anything got changed at all." Some said we should give the new FunTime a chance. Some said we didn't seem to have much of a choice.

Forty percent (estimated) loss of classmates' support for Rebellion: "Are we still supposed to do that Rebellion thing?" somebody asked Tommy. It's not like everybody is ready to give up, but some people are less intense about it now. We may need to start recruiting/advertising again.

ZERO percent loss of Jedi Council support for Rebellion. WE are all still in this!

ZERO percent agreement on what to do next.

Remi/Mara Jade: Okay, like I was saying last night . . . all we have to do is, when the teachers aren't looking, we take all the FunTime DVDs.

Sara: No way! That's stealing, and then we'd only be in more trouble.

Remi/Mara Jade: Where's Han Foldo? Let him talk. He'd do it.

Sara/Han Foldo: No, he says, "That's not my idea of courage. More like . . . suicide." I mean, seriously, Rabbski would know who it was immediately.

Amy: Yeah, I'm not doing it. Besides, they would just order more from Edu-Fun.

Remi/Mara Jade: All right, fine! Then what do you want to do?

Harvey: First, I want you to stop waving that obnoxious, noncanon puppet in my face!

Tommy/Foldy-Wan: Careful, Harvey. Don't let Rabbski turn us against each other!

Me (Mike/Mace): Does anyone have any less Dark Side ideas?

[Most of the rest of the ideas were MORE Dark Side, and I doubt the people really meant them.]

Tommy: Okay . . . I wanted to hear what everybody had to say first, but now I think it's time to ask Origami Yoda.

[Dwight was over by the magazine rack . . .

tying himself to the rack with the strings on
his hoodie.]

Tommy: Uh, what are you doing, Dwight?

Dwight: Tying myself to the magazine rack.

Tommy: Could you bring Origami Yoda over to
            the table? We need his advice.

Dwight: Sorry, but I'm tied to the magazine
            rack.

Tommy: Guys! You'll have to come over here.

[We went over there.]

Tommy: Okay, Origami Yoda. Rabbski seems to
            have us beat. What do we do now?

Origami Yoda: Hrmmm . . . Not your opponent she
            is. FunTime, Edu-Fun . . . the tests.
            These your opponents are, not Rabbski.

Harvey: This is just the same thing he told us
            a month ago!

Kellen: Would you relax, Harvey? Maybe he keeps
            saying it because it's true.

Tommy: Okay, Origami Yoda . . . that still
            doesn't tell us what to do.

Origami Yoda: Bad attitudes you have, she thinks.

Lance: Yeah, we know. She yelled that at us in the hall yesterday!

Origami Yoda: Prove her wrong you must!

Harvey: You want us to go around being happy about FunTime? That would kill me.

Origami Yoda: No! A lie that would be. Rabbski the Truth needs. Show her . . . the case file.

Tommy: What case file?

Origami Yoda: This one. The one you are making now. That these words will be in. Show her you must.

Tommy: No way!

Origami Yoda: MUST!

Harvey: Not this again.

Sara: Okay, look, I think we got our answer. Let's sit down and talk about it and leave Dwight to, uh, untie himself?

Amy: Okay, just to be clear . . . We kept a case file of basically everything we did to "disrupt the learning environment," and Origami Yoda wants

MERRY XMAS, MS. RABBSKI!

EVERYTHING WE'VE DONE WRONG IN ONE HADNY CASE FILE!

to give it to the person whose job is punishing people who "disrupt the learning environment."

Harvey: Yeah, and some of us added angry comments about that person.

Kellen: Not to mention rude doodles of that person.

Sara: If we do it, we have to take out Rhondella's chapter about the yearbook! She could get in huge trouble!

Quavondo: And my chapter, which is secret, anyway!

Amy: Yeah, I don't think I need her to read what I wrote!

Tommy: I can't remember if I wrote anything bad in the comments. Maybe I should erase those.

Kellen: Well, definitely print it out again without my pictures. Or that thing about the book reports.

Remi: And, Mike, don't write down that thing Mara Jade said a minute ago about stealing the DVDs.

EMPTY?

DWIGHT   OR   CAPTAIN DWIGHT?

Dwight: I think Origami Yoda was pretty clear.
           He wants you to show her the whole
           thing.

Tommy: Dwight . . . you're untied.

Dwight: Yes! Two minutes and thirty-seven
           seconds. A new record.

Tommy: And . . . uh . . . are you Dwight or
           Captain Dwight right now?

Dwight: [pulling a potato out of the hood of his
           hoodie] Neither. I'm a magic squirrel.

Harvey: Okay . . . All in favor of trusting
           the advice of Harry Squirreldini, say
           'Aye!'"

[No one says "Aye," not even Dwight. Personally,
I have ALWAYS followed Origami Yoda's advice
before. But I don't know, this time it just
doesn't seem right. Trust Rabbski? That's just
too much to ask! And the fact that the guy
asking it then began making his potato talk
to Yoda in a really high lady's voice didn't
help.]

[Argument resumes . . . goes nowhere . . .]

So the meeting ended without anyone agreeing to anything except NOT to show the case file to Rabbski. It's not like we decided to stop rebelling; we just couldn't decide how to continue rebelling.

So . . . is this the end of the Rebellion?

Harvey's Comment

⤳ of course it's not the end! There's another month of pain, agony, and a rapping calculator, and then next year a whole year of whatever this new Edu-Fun technological terror is going to be. Wheee!

My Comment: I think he meant the end of the case file. But I think we should keep it going until we win or lose . . . But right now I can't see how we can win when no one can agree on what to do next.

THE END?

AND SO THERE YOU HAVE IT, MS. RABBSKI.

YOU SAID THE REBELS HAVE BAD ATTITUDES,

BUT THE CASE FILE TELLS A DIFFERENT STORY.

TRUE, WE THOUGHT YOU WERE OUR OPPONENT . . .

BUT YOU THOUGHT WE WERE YOUR OPPONENTS.

YOU WANTED TO SQUASH THE REBELLION.

YOU HAVE BEEN ACTING LIKE EMPEROR PRINCIPALTINE.

SEARCH YOUR FEELINGS. YOU KNOW THIS IS TRUE.

BUT IT IS NOT TRUE ANYMORE. IS IT?

YOU HAVE READ THEIR CASE FILE, AND NOW YOU

UNDERSTAND THEM, RIGHT? YOU ARE READY TO HELP

THEM NOW, RIGHT?

SO I ASK ONE LAST TIME: HELP US

PRINCIPAL RABBSKI . . .

THIS IS OUR MOST

DESPERATE HOUR.

YOU'RE OUR ONLY HOPE

LOVE,

PRINCESS LABELMAKER

P.S. KEEP ME AND USE

ME AS A PUPPET AS NEEDED.

I MAY COME IN HANDY.

THE MYSTERY OF THE MISSING CASE FILE!!!!

BY TOMMY

Here's the chain of events:

Last night, Mike e-mailed me his transcript of our big meeting in the library yesterday. The one where we couldn't agree on whether or not to give the case file to Rabbski.

Actually, everybody did agree NOT TO DO IT. Everybody except Origami Yoda, that is.

And now the case file is missing.

Oh, wait, I forgot the chain of events:

Last night: Mike e-mails the transcript.

I print the transcript, put it in the case file folder, put the case file folder in my backpack.

This morning: I give the case file to Kellen to add doodles to the latest chapter. Kellen does a couple of doodles before homeroom. I see him stick the case file in his backpack, notice that he has already wrinkled up the new pages. How does he do it?

FULL

At lunch: Yesterday's argument about what to do next continues. Lance wants to look up the exact wording of things Origami Yoda said yesterday. Kellen looks in his backpack for the case file. It's not there.

MOTH

EMPTY

Probably in his locker, I figure. No, says Kellen. It can't be in his locker, because his locker is so jammed with stuff that it won't open. (This is not the first time this has happened to Kellen.)

MINE

Also at lunch: We ask Origami Yoda what happened to it. "Last place you saw it looked in have you?"

"Oh, for crying out loud," says Harvey. "Not that same lame advice again! I don't think he's even trying!"

"Actually, we do need to look for it before we panic," Amy says. "When DID you have it last, Kellen?"

"I put it in my bag in the library and then went straight to Mrs. Porterfield's for homeroom."

Right after lunch: We risk being late to Mr. Randall's class by run-walking down to Mrs. Porterfield's class to look. It's not there. And we ARE late to Mr. Randall's class. But he doesn't seem to care . . . about anything. Poor guy.

After school: Kellen, Mike, Harvey, and I look in every possible place it could be. It's not in any of them.

"Listen, guys, I'm SURE I put it in my backpack," says Kellen. "I never take it out in class. Only at home and in the library."

"It's pretty clear that somebody took it," says Mike. "But who?"

"And what are they going to do with it?" I ask.

"Erase Kellen's doodles, hopefully!" says Harvey.

"Not now, Harvey. I'm serious!"

"Well, it's pretty obvious what they're going to do with it. It has to be one of two things."

"Two things? I can only think of one," Mike says.

"Well, I can think of two," says Harvey. "One: Follow Origami Yoda's advice and give it to Rabbski. Or two: Hide it so that some idiot doesn't follow Origami Yoda's advice and give it to Rabbski."

"How do we know which one?" I ask.

"Easy," says Harvey. "If they hid it, then nothing changes."

"Yes, but what if they DID give it to Rabbski?"

"Oh, well, then she'll be calling us all into her office first thing in the morning so that she can wave the case file in our faces and declare us guilty of disrupting the learning environment in the first degree and then shoot us with Sith lightning while chuckling evilly."

Harvey's Comment

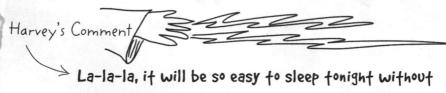

La-la-la, it will be so easy to sleep tonight without a worry in the world!

My Comment: I think Foldy-Wan is stuck on repeat, too: "I've got a bad feeling about this!"

WELL, I DO! WHAT DO YOU WANT ME TO SAY, FOR CRYING OUT LOUD ???

SUIT GUY

MS. RABBSKI CALLS US ALL TO HER OFFICE FIRST THING

BY MIKE

Place: Ms. Rabbski's office

Time: First thing

Attendees: All of us and Rabbski and a guy in a suit

Rabbski: Oh, boy, it's a little tight in here. See, Mr. Beckerman? I told you I needed a bigger office.

Mr. Beckerman: [chuckles]

Rabbski: Everyone, this is Charles Beckerman, superintendent of Lucas County schools.

Harvey: So . . . we meet again!

Mr. Beckerman: Oh? Oh, yes, you were the boy at
             one of our school board meetings about
             the . . . er, other boy.

Dwight: That was me, before I became a magic
           squirrel.

Mr. Beckerman: Aha . . . well . . .

Rabbski: Okay, let's get started before we all
           faint from the heat in here. First of
           all, I have to tell you, you definitely
           picked the right character for me.

[Note from me (Mike): I think I speak for almost
everybody when I say that our general reaction
to all of this was "Whut the Hutt is she talking
about?"]

[Then Ms. Rabbski holds up an origami—well,
probably kirigami—Princess Leia.]

Rabbski: I don't know if I would have listened to
           anybody but Leia. You know, I always wanted
           to be Leia when I was a kid. How about you,
           Mr. Beckerman? Did you want to be Luke?

Mr. Beckerman: I never watched *Star Trek*.

Harvey: *STAR TREK*? IT'S NOT *STA*—

Rabbski: Not right now, Harvey. Maybe we can
           loan him some *Star Wars* DVDs later.

           Anyway . . . I did listen to Leia.
           And I did read your case file. And, no,
           you're not in trouble.

           Just the opposite. Your file made me
           realize that FunTime just isn't the
           right thing for some of you.

           I mean, someone who can draw like
           Kellen and Remi needs an art class. And
           Cassie and Harvey need a drama coach.
           And Tommy and Sara need a LEGO team. And
           Dwight needs . . . well, something more
           interesting than Professor FunTime.

[Again, I think I speak for all of us when I say
we were all thinking, "Great jumping Jawas!"]

Rabbski: So last night I called Mr. Beckerman and
           I told him that some students simply
           are not benefiting from FunTime, because
           they already know the material—

Harvey: You can say that again!

129

Rabbski: Actually, I would like to say it for the first time—without being interrupted, Harvey. Now . . . I told Mr. Beckerman that some of you were not benefiting from FunTime and you needed a bigger challenge.

He agreed.

And he tells me we can actually make it happen on a limited basis right away. And then next year, it will be fully funded and last all year. Do you want to tell them about it, Mr. Beckerman?

Mr. Beckerman: Yes, thank you, Lougene . . . er, Ms. Rabbski. We have another pilot program over at Federle Middle School. It's called AR-GAP. Advanced . . . er, something . . . Program.

Basically, it's for the top few kids in each grade. The ones who probably don't need to review for the Standards tests and have special talents and interests to pursue.

Rabbski: What he's saying is that you'll have a class where you can draw comics, build LEGO robots, put on plays, whatever . . . and never have to watch FunTime again!

Harvey: YES!!!! [starts thrashing around]

Rabbski: Okay, Harvey, I know you're happy, but there's not quite enough room in here for a victory dance. Maybe we can all do one in the hall when we're done here.

[I felt like that weird-looking guy, Nien Nunb, who sits next to Lando in *Return of the Jedi* and is all like, "YABAYABAYABA," because he's so happy. In this case "yabayabayaba" means "YEE-HA! Goofing around in a special class for the rest of middle school!"]

Rabbski: And I almost forgot. The class would have the opportunity to take its own field trips.

Lance: To Craphole Plantation?

Rabbski: Er . . . no. And, Lance, let's remember

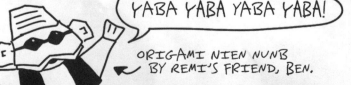

YABA YABA YABA YABA!

ORIGAMI NIEN NUNB
BY REMI'S FRIEND, BEN.

that we have a special visitor today who doesn't need to hear words like that. What I'm saying is, a field trip could probably be arranged to Washington, D.C. [By this point, I was looking for a Sharpie to draw a big smile on Mace Windu!]

Sara: Just a second . . . You say this is for the top students? Do you mean the best test scores?

Rabbski: Mostly, but other factors—especially creativity—will count, too. Don't worry, Sara, you're in. In fact, look around you. The people in this room are basically the members of the seventh-grade gifted class!

Mr. Beckerman: Of course, this year's test scores WILL matter when we select students for next year's gifted program. We expect all of you to drop this idea of getting low scores. We're counting on all of you to get the highest scores you can. You'll be helping the school and helping yourselves by guaranteeing yourselves a place in AR-GAP next year.

[Tommy held up Foldy-Wan Kenobi.]

Foldy-Wan: A generous offer. But one we cannot accept.

Rabbski, Mr. Beckerman, and Harvey: WHAT???!?!?!

Foldy-Wan: We have not fought this battle to win luxury for ourselves. Rather . . . we seek freedom and peace for everyone.

Harvey: Great, NOW he finally talks!

Mr. Beckerman: I don't understand. The puppet doesn't want to be in AR-GAP?

Harvey: [holding up Anakin] This puppet does! This puppet does!

Foldy-Wan: Don't let your feelings get in the way, Anakin. We have made a commitment to the Origami Rebel Alliance. A commitment not easily broken.

Anakin: Don't lecture me, Foldy-Wan. I can unfold you, old man!

Rabbski: BOYS! This is NOT helping you. Tommy,

please explain yourself. Do you want the special class or not?

Tommy: Well, I mean, we do. But we won't make a deal like that. We're only here because we got enough people to join so that you couldn't ignore us all.

So we can't make a deal unless it helps EVERYBODY.

Amy: Right! That means bringing back real classes for EVERYBODY.

Jen: And sports and cheerleading and chorus for EVERYBODY!

Lance: And a real field trip for EVERYBODY!

[Oh, yeah, I had forgotten about "everybody." Now I felt guilty. And bummed out all over again, because you could already see from Rabbski's and Beckerman's faces that "everybody" was going to lose.]

Mr. Beckerman: That . . . is not what we're offering. We are NOT scrapping the FunTime project, not until we see what effect it has on test scores. And we

expect the new Xtreme.Fun program to have an even bigger effect. Those test scores have GOT to come up! And you are all a part of that.

Tommy: No, we aren't . . . not while Professor FunTime and the Edu-Fun Empire still reign.

EMPEROR FUNTIME?

Mr. Beckerman: Okay, listen. I think you are confused. There is no Edu-Fun "Empire." It's just a company that makes tests and test-prep programs and—

Amy: Wait— They make the tests, too? And I suppose those also cost big bucks? So basically this company charges to teach us the test and then charges us to take the test? What's that got to do with—

Rabbski: [standing up] Okay, listen, I don't think we're getting anywhere. Mr. Beckerman, I'll let you get back to the central office, and I'll let these kids get back to class. And we'll give them some time to think about it.

WE'RE JUST TRYING TO BRING ORDER TO YOUR SCHOOL . . .

Sara: We don't need time to—

Rabbski: Sara! Not now. Head back to class,
          everyone, except Tommy. Would you wait
          outside in the office, please? I'd like
          another word with you.

Harvey's Comment

→ **Yeah, all right, you were right. And anyway . . . AR-GAP? I have a bad feeling about that! It's probably an Edu-Fun product!**

My Comment: Amy looked it up later. It is!
    Meanwhile, while you guys skipped off to class, I had to face Rabbski ALONE!

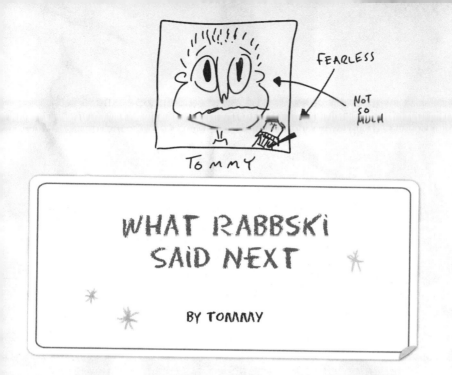

FEARLESS

NOT SO MUCH

TOMMY

WHAT RABBSKI SAID NEXT

BY TOMMY

Prepare to have your mind blown—well, unless you already heard me tell this story, which you probably did. But still . . . mind-blowing stuff ahead!

Rabbski didn't ask me to stay behind so that she could expel me, send me to CREF, punch me in the stomach, or even just yell at me.

Instead, she said, "Tommy, I'm impressed."

And I was like, "WHAT THE HUTT?" (I didn't actually say that out loud. I didn't say anything!)

OKAY, PLEASE STOP SAYING THAT NOW . . .

But I guess I did smile, because she said, "I didn't say I was PLEASED, just impressed."

But then she smiled a bit, too.

"Well, maybe I am pleased. I don't know how to fix this mess yet, but . . . you were right. A special class for some of you wasn't going to do it."

"A class like that WOULD be awesome," I said, just in case she hadn't understood. "But, you know, shouldn't everybody have an awesome class instead of a totally unawesome one?"

This time she laughed—well, a snort-laugh.

"'Unawesome'? Don't you mean 'nostrul'? That's what Princess Labelmaker told me."

"What else did she tell you?" I asked.

"All kinds of stuff! I read your whole case file . . . No, relax, nobody is getting in trouble. Princess Labelmaker really opened my eyes. And today you opened them even further."

That's when I realized this wasn't going to be an argument. We had done it. Princess Labelmaker—and whoever made her—had done it.

Somehow we got the Emperor to come back from the Dark Side. Or maybe Origami Yoda was right and she never was the Emperor in the first place. Either way: We won!

WE WON!

"So," I asked, "does this mean you're going to cancel FunTime?"

"Honestly, Tommy, I'm not sure what to do.

"As the princess would say, 'It's not over yet!' I guess our next step is going to be to convince the superintendent and the school board. I knew we weren't going to get anywhere with the superintendent today. That's why I sent him back to his office. Plus, I'm not exactly sure what we're trying to convince them of, much less how to do it. We need a plan of attack!"

"Attack?" I said. She was starting to sound like Mon Mothma!

WELL, IT'S ABOUT TIME I GOT A MENTION!!!

"Sorry. Poor choice of words," she said.

139

WHO? LITTLE OL' ME?

"No, 'attack' sounds good to me," I said. "Gizmo needs to die!"

She sighed and sat down.

"I can't argue that one anymore. I've hated that 'nostrul' calculator from the first time I saw him! But . . ." And she smiled. Not an evil smile, but a nice smile. A real smile. "Hate to the Dark Side leads, right? We've got to figure out how to fix this mess the Jedi way."

And she picked up the Princess Leia puppet and said, "I only hope that when the data's analyzed, a weakness can be found!"

Harvey's Comment

That was a quality Leia quote! But are you sure we can trust her? What if this is another one of her tricks to kill more time?

My Comment: I am 100 percent sure we can trust her! You would be, too, if you had talked to her.

Also, I asked her about Princess Labelmaker. She

said she honestly didn't KNOW who gave it to her. She found the puppet and the case file on her desk. And the case file had all these black labels stuck to it that spelled out little notes and stuff.

She said reading the case file was one of the highlights of her career and no one was going to get in any trouble because of it!

She gave me the case file back, by the way, so at least we have our case file together again, even if it's not a secret case file anymore.

Harvey's Second Comment

Whew! Thank Jabba we got the case file back. Just imagine if we had lost all of those precious doodles!

YEAH! ESPECIALLY THIS ONE!

YUKKA BAWUCKA!

PRINCESS LABELMAKER

PRINCESS LABELMAKER *(FINALLY!) AND THE SCHOOL BOARD MEETING

BY TOMMY

After that, Ms. Rabbski talked to all of us a bunch of times. But she didn't call us into her office; she actually came to the library and sat down and talked with us. It was weird.

We mostly agreed on what we wanted—there were a couple things that she said would never happen—and then discussed how we would try to convince the school board to end FunTime and restore everything else.

The school board had a meeting scheduled for

MEDIA CENTER

THIS MEANS "LIBRARY"

that Thursday night, and the superintendent told Rabbski they would be discussing some FunTime stuff. This turned out to be a real understatement. They were going to do a lot more than "discuss" it. They had some seriously Dark Side plans . . . but I'll get to that in a minute.

First, Rabbski called all our parents again.

This time she told them she could use their support at the school board meeting that was coming up. She told them she was trying to replace the singing calculator with real classes.

My dad was like, "So you're in trouble again?"

"No," I said. "Rabbski is on our side now."

"So . . . then I don't have to go the meeting?"

So he didn't go, and my mom had a Swim Club Boosters meeting, so she didn't go.

Kellen's mom gave me a ride to the high school, where they have the school board meetings in the library.

When we got there, we sat at a table near the front with Dwight, Sara, Amy, Lance, Quavondo, Murky, Remi, and James Suervo.

Mike didn't come. He was afraid someone would say something that would get his mom worked up again, so he talked her out of it. He gave me the Holocron to take notes in and was really fussy about me not messing it up. Never mind that I am already putting together this case file.

At the two tables behind us, our parents sat with some of our teachers: Mr. Randall, Mr. Howell, Miss Bauer, and Mrs. Porterfield. I was glad my parents weren't there. It makes me nervous when parents and teachers start chatting. Quavondo's little sister was sitting back there, too, texting or something. After all this time, she still hadn't joined the Rebellion.

The meeting was held at the same place where I went back in October when Rabbski was trying to get Dwight kicked out. It was hard to believe we were all there on the same side this time.

I wonder if she changed or if we changed? Or maybe FunTime is just so evil that everybody wanted to fight it. Or maybe she understood us better now.

When we walked in, someone handed us each a sheet of paper that said, "Agenda." I skimmed down and saw us at number four.

"Four: Consideration of AR-GAP pilot program for gifted students at McQuarrie Middle School."

"That's us," I said.

"Uh huh . . . did you see number three?" asked Sara.

"Three: Presentation from Edu-Fun Educational Products. Purchase of Xtreme.Fun program for elementary schools and remaining middle schools."

"They're actually thinking of getting FunTime for other schools, too!" said Sara.

"Well, at least we won't be in the Sarlacc pit alone anymore," said Harvey.

"We have to win tonight," said Foldy-Wan (me). "Or other school systems will suffer the same fate."

"Our mission . . . even graver than we thought," said Origami Yoda.

"Oh, Dwight," his mother barged in. "I didn't mean for you to bring the Yoda here. I don't think it's such a good idea to antagonize Ms. Rabbski with . . ."

"Don't worry, Mrs. Tharp," said Ms. Rabbski, who was walking back to the table after talking to the superintendent. "I brought mine, too." And she held up Princess Labelmaker.

Then she came to our table.

"Don't forget, this is a diplomatic mission . . . Use your manners!" said the princess. "And . . . may the Force be with US!"

LET'S DO THIS!

Let's just stop and think about that for a
second: Our principal talking to us through
a hand puppet. This is the same person who
tried to ban origami from our school once!
Cray-zee!!!

"Look, Ani," said Pad-mé/Murky to Harvey/
Anakin, "it's our little girl, Leia, all
grown up!"

"Would you stop it?" said Harvey. "I—"

But then the suit guy, Mr. Beckerman, who
had come to our school, pulled a microphone
in front of himself and started the meeting.

We started with the Pledge of Allegiance
just like last time. And we, the rebels,
were feeling it!

"Liberty and justice for all!"

Then there was a moment of silence, and
then the meeting started.

Suit Guy: This is the time for public comment.
We'll ask each speaker to limit
their comments to five minutes.

Now, while we are always interested in hearing from students, a quick head count tells me that if you each speak for five minutes, we will be here until midnight.

And I believe many of you are here to speak to the same issue?

Most of us: Yes!

Suit Guy: Ahem, yes. Well, we're very appreciative of your enthusiasm. But I will remind you that this is not a pep rally. Also, I'm going to ask—in the interest of saving time—that one student be chosen to summarize your group's position, so that we need only hear it once.

Rabbski had prepared us for this. So I had written up a single five-minute–if–I–talked-fast speech.

I stood up to talk, but Suit Guy interrupted me!

CORA   IONAPPRACTICA HATICA MATHEMATICA WHOO BOO LALA TABAR BUG

148

Suit Guy: First, however, we'd like to welcome a very distinguished guest, Dr. Karl Blonsky, CEO and founder of Edu-Fun Educational Products.

We had NOT been prepared for this!

I half expected to see Professor FunTime stand up with Gizmo and try to get the school board to rap about FunTime.

But this Edu-Fun guy wasn't the Professor. He was just some middle-aged dude wearing the exact same suit as Suit Guy.

He started yammering away with all these weird words: "Norm-referenced longitudinal data quartiles. Receptive metrics curriculum benchmarking objectives."

We couldn't understand a word he was saying, but he was obviously speaking some kind of school board language, because they all seemed to love him.

"Common Core proficiency outliers," he would say, and they would all nod their

MALA GOOBA TOOBA ROOBA MOOBURGER HINEY

heads. Sometimes he didn't even use words.

"APPR CCSS RTI SSI 504 EOG."

Suit Guy thought this was the best thing he'd ever heard in his life!

And Dr. Edu-Fun handed them really fancy brochures and booklets and tote bags and stuff. They kept nodding their heads.

"I'd love to show you a short film about FunTime," he said. "Let me get the projector going."

On one of the tables he had a laptop computer and one of those projector things. He started it up and asked for someone to turn out the lights. The "short film" was really just a long commercial.

It was all dreamy, like with tinkly music and shots of happy, happy children. And then the children looked right at the camera and said crazy stuff about how great FunTime was.

"Traitors!" hissed Harvey.

"They're just actors, shhh!" said Amy.

Anyway, the video made FunTime sound like the best thing ever. It ended with a kid going, "Mommy! I did my best on the test!" and hugging his mom. And the school board members actually clapped!

"Oh, wug," said Sara.

"We're doomed . . . again!" said C-3PO/Lance.

JABBA THE PUPPETT

RETURN OF THE JABBA

BY TOMMY

Dr. Edu-Fun had a smug look on his face when the lights came back on.

"So, as you can see," he said, "kids and educators agree . . . FunTime turns kids into great test takers!

"Tests do not make one great!"

"WHAT?" said Suit Man and Dr. Edu-Fun at the same time.

"Tests do not make one great!" It was Origami Yoda!

"Young man," said Suit Man. "Would you

please sit down and put that . . . whatever
it is . . . away?"

"It's Yoda!" barked Harvey, standing up
next to Dwight with Anakin. "Don't tell me
you don't know who Yoda is. Oh, I forgot,
he's not on the test, so he doesn't matter."

"I do know who Yoga is. Er, Yoda . . . But
he certainly has no place at this meeting!"

"ACTUALLY . . . HE DOES!"

It was Rabbski.

Now she was standing up, too.

"Origami Yoda does have a place here . . .
along with Dwight and these other amazing
students . . ."

She pointed at us and we all held up our
puppets and cheered, just to show the school
board that we were not like the actors in
that video.

"They have been trying to tell me for
months that FunTime doesn't work the way it
does in that video. It took me a while, but
I finally listened. And now . . . we're here

153

to tell you that we are done with the FUNTIME worksheets, we're done with the FUNTIME TV shows, and most of all we're done with the moronic singing calculator!"

So much for the "diplomatic mission." Rabbski was letting them have it!

"Lougene, please!" said Suit Man. "Not only are you interrupting our guest, but now you are being rude."

"Rude? No, just descriptive. And you'd know that if you had ever taken one of these tests or watched the stupid videos. What would you say if you had to listen to this every day? Hit it, Howell!"

We turned to see Mr. Howell messing around with Dr. Edu-Fun's laptop.

He looked up guiltily.

"Lougene? You knew?" he said.

"Yeah, I figured it out," said Rabbski. "I assume you have another video ready for us? Good . . . Now, hit it . . ."

Howell held up Jabba, let out a big "Mwa-ha-ha-ha," and then hit a button.

MWAHAHA

"FunTime Style" came blaring out of the speakers!

"FUNTIME! Gonna have a FUNTIME!"

Oh, man, it was loud!

Somebody turned the lights out, and we could see Professor FunTime and the singing calculator ten feet tall on the screen.

"GONNA GETCHA READY!"

Howell must have edited together a greatest-hits supercut of Professor FunTime and Gizmo and smuggled it in on a USB drive or something.

"FUNdamentals! Get them in Focus! You'll be a test-taking WIZARD! Hocus Pocus!"

The school board members were obviously saying stuff like "Really!" or maybe even "How rude," but we couldn't hear them.

"Mr. Howell? What are you doing? Please return to your seat!" boomed Suit Guy into his microphone.

Howell pulled out a tiny Salacious Crumb and squealed, "Whatever you say, boss! HA-HA-HA-HA-HA!"

Then he went back to his seat but left the song running! And running . . . and running . . .

"Won't you take me to . . . FUNTime Town!"

Dr. Edu-Fun kept pointing at the computer with his little clicker device. The music wouldn't stop!

"Every second, every minute, will help you Focus on the FUNdamentals!"

Finally he gave up and walked back to his computer, and after a minute he finally got the song to shut off.

Amy stood up and waved R2-D2 and some papers at the school board. "In case you didn't understand, THAT is the, quote-unquote, educational program you paid $45,619 for!"

"And if anybody is wondering," said Murky with Pad-mé, "the breakdancing-dictionary videos are actually worse!"

"Please be quiet!" said Suit Guy. "Dr. Blonsky, I apologize for these interruptions . . . Please continue."

THAT WAS HURTFUL . . . .

"Well . . . ," said Dr. Edu-Fun, "the videos are . . . uh, only part of an interactive package that also includes—"

"WORKSHEETS!" we all said at once.

"Well, yes, interactive sample tests . . . Ahem. But what I would really like to point out to the board and the parents and educators in attendance is that the video clip you've just seen was from our previous FunTime learning program. We collected feedback about the videos and have created an entirely new and richly interactive, Standards-focused, Common Core-based HD digital video series. The package that you're considering tonight would include this new—and I would say much improved—digital learning experience."

NEW. -AND, - still not IMPROVED-

He looked so smug . . . He thought he had us beat! But he had underestimated the nerdiness level of Mr. Lance Alexander!

"OH, REALLY?" yelled Lance, completely forgetting to be a polite protocol droid like C-3PO. "I find it interesting that you call it

O, RLY?

THE
BALDY
CAP...

SMITHSONIAN MUSEUM

'much improved' . . . because Tevon Riley, the actor who portrays Professor FunTime, recently sent out this tweet: 'Can't believe I'm putting the baldy cap back on to do another "educational" series—and somehow it's even worse than the last one!'"

"Excuse me!" said Suit Guy.

"One second," said Lance. "Then the guy who does the voice acting for Gizmo the singing calculator tweeted back: 'Tell me about it. Haven't we destroyed the souls of enough children yet? #WhatAboutTheChildren? #HateGizmo.'"

EVEN ME DOESN'T LIKE ME!

Suit Guy stood up and slammed his hand down on the table.

"I'm going to have to insist that these interruptions stop! Now, you students need to wait your turn or leave. Which is it going to be?"

And then he put on this big show of apologizing to Dr. Edu-Fun, who put on a big show of acting like nothing had gone wrong at all. He reminded me of the car salesman who sold my dad that minivan with the bad engine.

"All right . . . ," said Suit Man. "Now . . . if a student representative would like to address the board. I feel I need to remind you AGAIN that this is not a pep rally and that your remarks should be limited to five minutes."

STILL NO PEP!

"Dr. Edu-Fun got twelve minutes . . . BEFORE he was interrupted!" Kellen announced, holding up his watch. "I timed it."

Suit Man glared. His eyes looked exactly like Darth Maul's!

"Just sayin'," said Kellen.

Harvey's Comment

Well played, Kellen!

My Comment: Yeah, well played, everybody!

But now it was my turn . . . and I was scared. Really scared. Suit Guy and the rest of the school board looked like they were ready to clobber me already, and I hadn't even said a word. And the speech I had written seemed really lame. And didn't seem to really answer all the baloney that Dr. Edu-Fun had said.

Dwight elbowed me. I looked over.

"Let fear defeat you do not," Origami Yoda said. "Foldy-Wan is fearless, as you must also be."

"And may the Force be with you," said Dwight.

FOLDY — WAN

THE VOICE OF FOLDY-WAN

BY TOMMY

I held up Foldy-Wan, and I was just drawing breath to begin my speech when one of the school board members—the old dude who I think is a retired principal—jumped up from his table and came right at me.

"NO!" he said really rudely. "There has been altogether too much foolishness already tonight. We may have to listen to you, but we are NOT going to listen to a puppet show."

And he grabbed Foldy-Wan off my finger and stomped back to his chair.

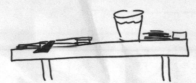

I watched as he put Foldy-Wan facedown on the table.

"You may continue," he said. He was so smug about it, and the other board members were so smugly approving of it, that Murky will have to invent a new word to describe that amount of smugness.

For a second I thought, "What am I going to do without Foldy-Wan?"

And then I heard him. Inside my head!

"The Force will be with you, Tommy."

No joke. I mean, I heard him REALLY, for REAL.

"Forget the speech. Trust your feelings . . ."

I took another breath. And then I said very, very calmly, "I had a whole thing to read to you here. I was going to tell you our whole case file. And all about how awful FunTime is. And how much we all hate it.

"But this is bigger than that.

"Here's all I ask of you.

"Think about everything you have taken

away from us: a field trip to Washington, JV sports, our chances to win the LEGO League, home ec, art class, band, drama, and a ton of other things we wanted to do.

"How can a school be better without those things?

"It might be better for Edu-Fun. Of course, they'll want you to think that their programs and their tests made it better. That way you'll keep giving them money.

"It might even be better for you, the school board. You're going to look at a number that Edu-Fun sends you. And if that number is a couple of points higher than the last time Edu-Fun sent you a number, then you're going to say that you made the school better.

"But it won't be better.

"Three extra points from Edu-Fun just doesn't equal all of that other stuff. Ten points? Thirty points? No. The points mean nothing to us, but those other things did.

"So . . . we're not going to give you the points. We're not going to bust our butts on Edu-Fun's tests so that Edu-Fun can show you the three points.

"You want to know if the rip-off FunTime program was a success?

"You can listen to us now . . . or you can find out when you get the results. But I can tell you now what the results are going to be . . . Because WE are the results!

"And WE are the Origami Rebellion!"

Harvey's Comment

I am so embarrassed to admit this, but . . . I was one of the people cheering.

RABBSKI + PRINCESS L.

RABBSKI'S MOMENT

BY TOMMY

The nasty guy who had taken Foldy-Wan still had his smug look.

"Well, young man, you certainly talk big. It's easy for you to say you'll blow off the tests. Perhaps you didn't know that if you flunk the tests, you may flunk your grade. Would you still be talking so big if you had to repeat the—"

"Actually, that won't be happening," said Ms. Rabbski, standing up.

"And why not?" asked Nasty Guy.

"If you recall," she said, "the resolution—which the school board passed—says that if a student fails the test, it is the principal's decision if they also fail the grade. Well, I've decided that no student will be punished because of his or her test score . . ."

She let that sink in a second and then said, "And I've made a few other decisions, too.

"I believe that McQuarrie is a great school, but these kids are right: We seem to have lost our focus.

"So as principal of McQuarrie, I am making the decision to suspend PERMANENTLY the FunTime pilot project."

Almost everybody: "YAY!"

Suit Man: "On what grounds?"

"Because," she said, "it is a distraction to the learning environment!"

We started cheering, but Rabbski waved at us to hush up.

"Though I was reluctant to go against the school board, enough is enough. I'm going to do everything a principal can do to get the learning environment back in shape. I'm going to restore every elective class I can. I'm going to let the band play and the wrestlers wrestle and the cheerleaders cheer and the LEGO club . . . uh, LEGO. And I'm going to get the drama club a budget and a coach . . . even if I have to coach them myself.

"Basically, we're going to have a gifted class for every kid in the school . . . And, no," she said, turning to Dr. Edu-Fun, "we don't need an Edu-Fun product to do it!"

Ms. Rabbski started to walk back to her seat. We cheered.

Chewbacca roared, "Hhhurgg hhhurgg!" And then Han Foldo shouted, "Chewie said 'FIELD TRIP!' Don't forget the field trip!"

"Oh, yeah . . . ," said Rabbski, turning back to the school board. "We're going on a field trip. And I don't mean to Craphole Plantation, either. I'm taking these kids on a real field trip. They earned it."

YOU CAN KEEP THE COOKIES, DARK SIDE!

origami Anakin was so blown away by all this that he would like to announce that he is NOT going to go to the Dark Side and become Darth Paper.

My Comment: I'm still amazed by Ms. Rabbski. Whoever gave her that Princess Labelmaker thing knew what they were doing! We cheered until Suit Man got all ugly again.

The school board didn't cheer. Instead they did a lot of moaning and groaning about "state guidelines" and "federal mandates."

But in the end they voted 5—4 to "table the Xtreme. Fun purchase, pending further review."

Mr. Randall said that's their way of throwing something into the Sarlacc pit.

"It's gone. They'll never mention it again," he said. "BUT . . . we'll have to keep an eye on them and make sure they don't sign us up for something worse."

Worse than FunTime? Impossible! (But terrifying!)

DON'T WORRY, PROFESSOR . . . NOW WE CAN HAVE XTREME.FUN _TOGETHER_ AS WE ARE SLOWLY DIGESTED OVER A _THOUSAND YEARS!_

THE REPORTER

WE MADE THE NEWS

BY SARA

When the meeting was over, this newspaper reporter asked us some questions and took a picture of our puppets. The next morning my grandma called to tell me I was in the paper and that she was proud of me!

Here's the article:

NOW, LET'S RAP SOME MORE!

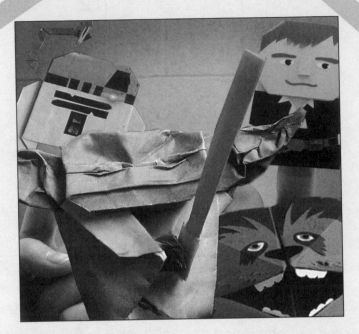

Test-Prep Brouhaha at Lucas Co. School Board

Vinton—*Star Wars* puppets faced off against a singing calculator at last night's Lucas County Board of Education meeting.

At issue is McQuar-rie Middle School's use of classroom videos to help students prepare for state standardized tests. The school board was considering wheth-er to expand the program, which costs nearly $50,000 per school, countywide.

However, the school board took no action on the measure after students—and their *Star Wars* puppets—voiced their discontent with the program.

McQuarrie Middle School had the lowest test scores in the county last year, but students say the classroom videos aren't helping.

"The [videos] are absolute garbage," said seventh grader Lance Alexander, who brought a finger puppet of *Star Wars* robot C-3PO to the meeting.

"The puppets are sort of a symbol for us," said Sara Bolt, another seventh grader, who had two puppets: Chewbacca and Han Solo, heroes of the original *Star Wars* movies. "We are sort of like the rebels from *Star Wars*," explained Bolt, "and [the] FunTime [program] is the Empire."

The students' principal, Lougene Rabbski, even had her own puppet version of Princess Leia, which she waved about during a passionate speech of her own.

She told the board that not only does she not support the continuation of the test-preparation program next year, but she actually plans to cut the pilot program short this year. Rabbski, who declined to comment for this article, also told the school board that she would not prevent students with low test scores from passing on to the next grade.

A teacher, Gorman Howell, played a clip from a video that is part of the test-prep program. It featured a man in a lab coat and an animated calculator singing, dancing, and possibly rapping. Reaction to the video was mixed.

"FunTime is our most popular product," said Dr. Karl Blonsky, CEO and founder of Edu-Fun Educational Products, the makers of the FunTime test-prep videos under consideration. He said he was unaware of any complaints about the videos from other school systems.

The school board also met in a closed session to discuss "personnel matters."

"Unaware"... Yeah, right. That guy would be unaware of a mynock sucking on his forehead!

My Comment: That last little bit about the "closed session?" That was BIG! HUGE!!!! We just didn't know it at the time. Well, Sara did . . .

HOW DO YOU FEEL ABOUT ACORNS, DOGS, THE DIGESTIVE TRACT, KIRIGAMI, AND ROTTA, ZIRO, AND JABBA?

I LIKE NUTS, MUTTS, GUTS, CUTS, AND HUTTS!

CAN I QUOTE YOU ON THAT?

SARA

RETURN OF THE RABBSKI . . .

BY SARA

Okay, while you guys were all outside YubNubbing about our victory, I realized something . . .

Rabbski had gone out on a limb for us. Way out! Maybe TOO FAR out.

I mean, if you were the school board and a school employee talked to you like that, wouldn't you want to fire them?

So, I went back to ask her if that was a possibility and if we needed to form a Rebel Alliance to Save Rabbski!

A few weeks ago it would have been hard to believe we would even consider such a thing. But after what

MASCOT?

she has done for us, I know we would come together for her if we had to!

But we don't have to!

The meeting was still going on, but they were on agenda item #8: Considering request from Federle M.S. Custodial Staff to change supply vendors. (In reference to recent Floor Wax Concerns.)

I was surprised to see the Edu-Fun guy talking again. I was afraid he was going to try to get them to buy Xtreme.Fun again, but he was actually talking about floor wax. (Does Edu-Fun sell *everything*?)

YES...

WAX TIME

Anyway, I whispered to Ms. Rabbski:

"Are you going to lose your job?"

She tapped her finger on the agenda: #12: CLOSED SESSION to discuss personnel matters.

"What?" I whispered too loud and Suit Guy glared at me.

"Let's go into the hall," whispered Ms. Rabbski.

When we got out there and the door had shut, she said, "Wow, that was some meeting, huh?"

"Yeah," I said. "But was it a big mistake? Are they going to fire you in that closed meeting?"

HI! I'M SHINY, THE SINGING MOP!

WUG!

"No," she said. "But they are going to accept my resignation."

THAT WAS HURTFUL!

"RESIGNATION??????"

"Shhh" she shhhhed. "Yes, Sara, this whole thing—and I don't just mean the Rebellion—I mean Dwight's suspension and banning the origami and the stupid FunTime show and selling bad popcorn and everything . . . The whole thing has made me realize I have the wrong job."

"But you're a great principal! You proved that just now!"

"Well, that's nice of you to say," she said. "But truthfully, I haven't enjoyed any of it . . . well, until I got to say 'Craphole Plantation.' That was fun."

We both laughed, although mine was more of a nervous I-can't-believe-she-said-it-again laugh.

"No," she said. "I had a lot more fun as a teacher."

"You were a teacher?"

"Oh, yes—math. And, believe it or not, I think kids actually used to like me."

"I think I would like you as a teacher," I said.

POP CORN

176

I CAN'T BELIEVE SHE SAID IT EITHER!

THAT IS REALLY #!@?% INAPPRO-PRIATE!

"Well, you'll have a chance to find out."

"Wha—"

"That's the other thing we'll discuss with #12. Ms. Liversedge, the eighth-grade math teacher, is leaving at the end of the school year, so . . ."

"So you're going to be our math teacher next year?"

"Yep! Your drama coach, too! And you have Origami Yoda to blame."

I gave her a hug. I felt like she deserved a hug, and I knew none of you boys were going to do it. So I gave her a big Origami Rebel Alliance hug from all of us.

Harvey's Comment

Math teacher, huh? Well, since I get straight A's in math, we should get along fine. Of course, if you're the kind of student who has problems with math . . . it could bring out her Sith side again!

My Comment: Uh-oh . . .

TOMMY

THE POST-FUNTIME ERA

BY TOMMY

So we've been back in our elective classes for about a week.

Some of the classes, like Kellen's art class, are a little strange. The art teacher has gotten another job somewhere else, so Mr. Howell is teaching the art class! I thought Kellen was going to freak, but he said the experience of having Mr. Howell teach art is so weird that it is giving him great material for a story. He's taking notes, and he says he's going to write a graphic novel

JUST SHUT UP
AND PAINT
THE FLOWER!

based on the whole thing and become famous. He might.

(By the way, Ms. Bolton relented and gave him a C+ for his *Fangbone* book report, so he's not failing English, and his mother lifted his punishment just in time for him to see the season finale of *Doctor Who*.)

The band teacher came back, but the chorus teacher wouldn't. So guess who Ms. Rabbski hired to be the substitute for the rest of the year?

I'll give you two hints: He can sing, and so can his monkey.

LA-LA-#!@%

Meanwhile, the LEGO robots class I signed up for is awesome! Mostly because Mr. Randall is a fun teacher, LEGOS in general are stooky, and of course . . . Sara is in the class!

One day Sara and I were at the back counter working on our robot, Crookshanks2000, and I was having trouble getting it to do anything—he doesn't do much even when he's working

I'M SO TIRED ...

179

right, but right then he was just sort of twitching—and I said, "I didn't realize LEGO robots were so hard to make. I thought you just sort of put them together and they worked."

"Yeah, well, that's why there's a class for it, silly!"

And she leaned over . . . and put her hands on my arm . . . and I think she was about to kiss me when . . .

"AHEM!"

We whirled around to see Ms. Rabbski standing in the doorway.

"If everyone has finished with their public displays of affection—which are against school handbook policy—I've brought your field trip permission slips, Mr. Randall."

"Thank you, Ms. Rabbski," said Mr. Randall, taking the stack of papers.

Can you believe what is going on here? I mean, look at where I was a year ago—a loser—and look at where I am now—almost getting

WHEW! RABBISKI GOT THERE JUST IN TIME!

NOW SHE'S MY NEW HERO!

kissed in robot class! And just a month and a
half ago there wasn't even a LEGO robots class.
There was only FunTime.

But Origami Yoda and Dwight changed all
that.

And actually, this time I helped, too,
with Foldy-Wan (who I got back from Nasty
Guy). And everybody and their puppets.

We haven't taken the tests yet, and we
haven't exactly figured out whether we'll try
to pass them, fail them, or what.

But Ms. Rabbski has hung up a new banner,
and I actually like this one:

"McQuarrie Middle School Students Are the
BEST in the GALAXY!"

And it has Princess Labelmaker and a bunch
of other characters we made for her glued to
it.

So, basically, she's not obsessed with the
tests anymore . . . so we aren't, either.

NO FAIR!

WE GOT LEFT OFF THE BANNER, DUDE!

W4H!

SCHOOL MASCOT

ME TOO!

The thing we ARE excited about now is our field trip. We fought hard for it and won it and now we get to enjoy it. And I plan to enjoy it more than anybody! Because this year I'll be sitting on the bus with Sara instead of Harvey and everything is just going to be stooky fizz-pop waffles with plastic dinosaurs on top!

Or not.

See, I was saying something like this at lunch, and Origami Yoda started to say something. I could tell it was in his scary warning voice.

But Dwight goes, "No, Yoda . . . don't tell him. They'll find out, anyway . . ."

I guess we will.

Harvey's Comment

Um . . . aren't you forgetting something?

Who STOLE the case file? Who gave it to Rabbski? Who WAS Princess Labelmaker??????

My Comment: Tut-tut, Harvey. I can't believe you never figured it out. It's obvious.

Who would sit around and click out all those letters onto labels? It must have taken forever!

Who would actually think that a labelmaker is "cool"?

Who could make an origami Princess Leia that good? With hair buns and everything?

Who wanted to be part of the Rebellion but couldn't be because he was scared of getting in trouble again?

And who actually told us to give the case file to Rabbski before Princess L. even got involved?

That's right . . . Dwight!

THAT'S CAPTAIN DWIGHT!

Permission Slip

McQuarrie seventh graders will be traveling to Washington, D.C., on May 17, to tour national monuments and explore the Smithsonian Institution's museums.

The cost per student will be $65, and each student may bring $10 to $20 to purchase a souvenir and supper from a fast-food restaurant on the return visit.

No cell phones or digital cameras. (Disposable cameras are preferred for students wishing to take photos.)

No public displays of affection.

No sodas.

No orange-colored snacks or drinks.

No peanuts (due to allergies).

No ORIGAMI! (Origami has been a fun part of our school year, but it is not appropriate for a field trip to our nation's capital, where we will be representing our school, county, and state.)

Chartered buses from Harmon's Tours will load PROMPTLY at 6 a.m. in the MMS upper parking lot. Please be on time.

Please sign and detach the permission slip below:

— — — — — — — — — — — — —

My child _____ has my permission to travel to Washington, D.C. My child understands the importance of following the rules and instructions given by school staff and chaperones. My child agrees to follow the rules listed above.

_____
(Signature of parent/guardian)

HOW TO FOLD
Princess
Leia!

INSTRUCTIONS BY KELLEN!

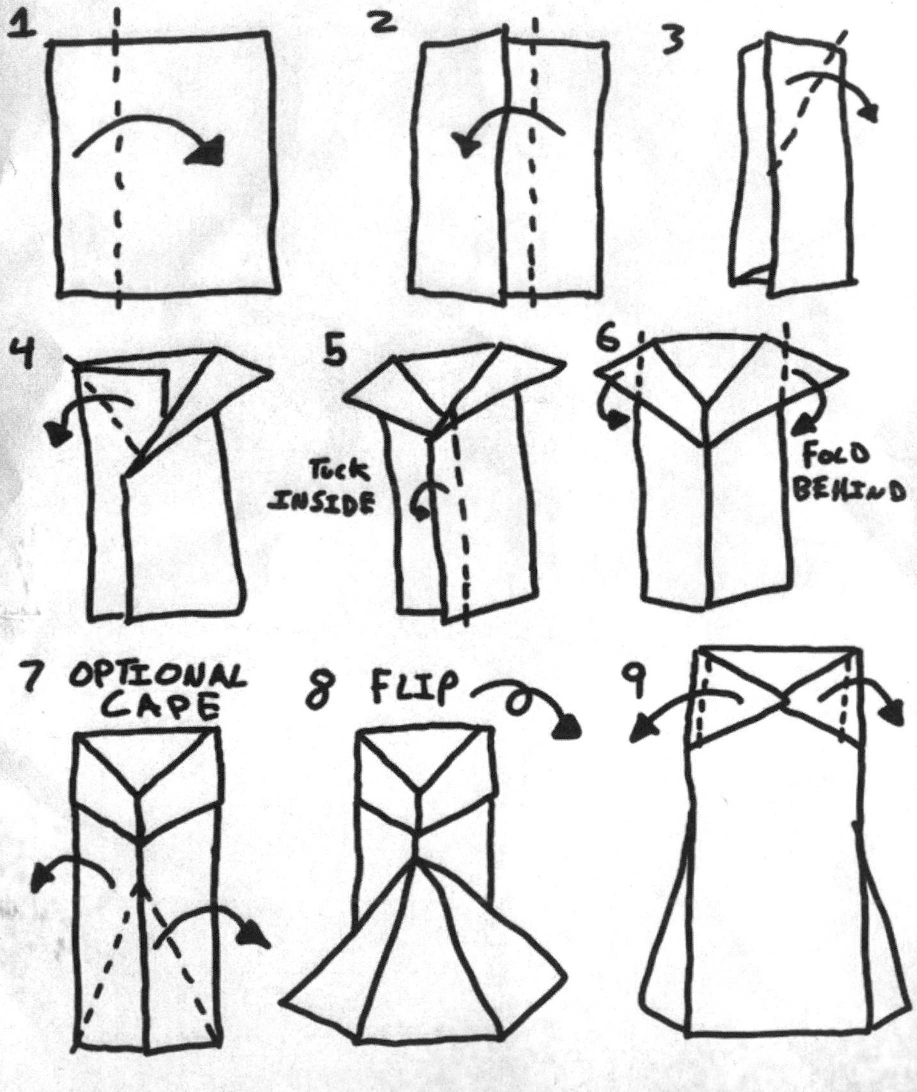

1

2

3

4

5 TUCK INSIDE

6 FOLD BEHIND

7 OPTIONAL CAPE

8 FLIP

9

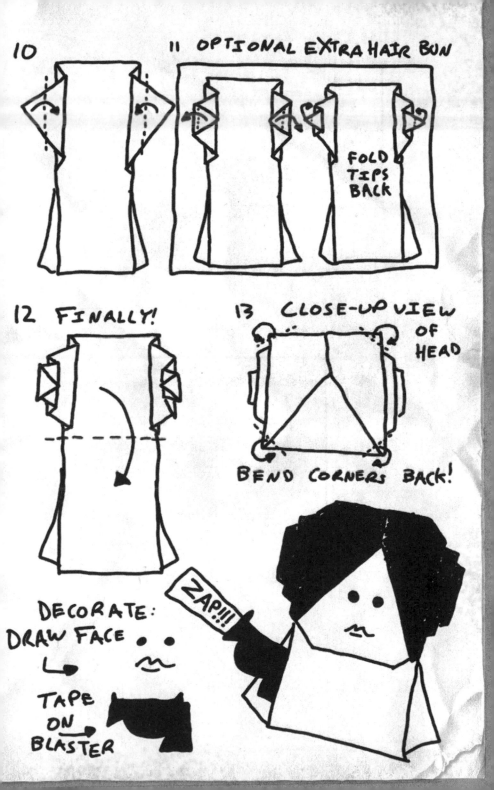

10

11 OPTIONAL EXTRA HAIR BUN

FOLD TIPS BACK

12 FINALLY!

13 CLOSE-UP VIEW OF HEAD

BEND CORNERS BACK!

DECORATE:
DRAW FACE

TAPE ON BLASTER

ZAP!!!

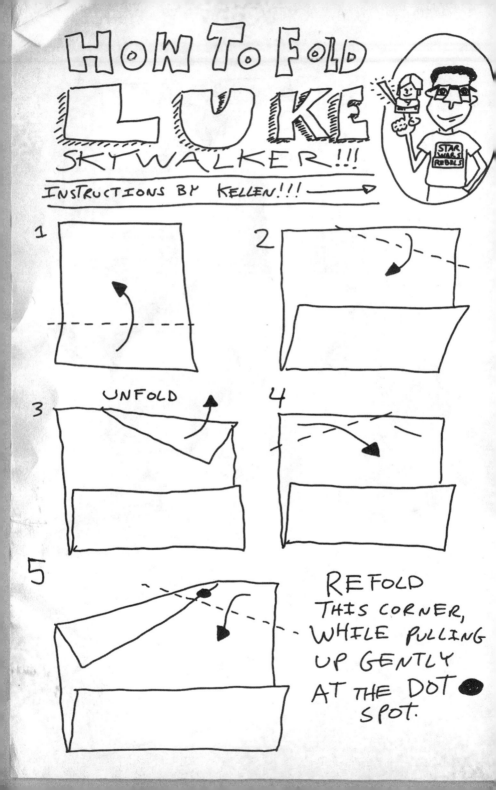

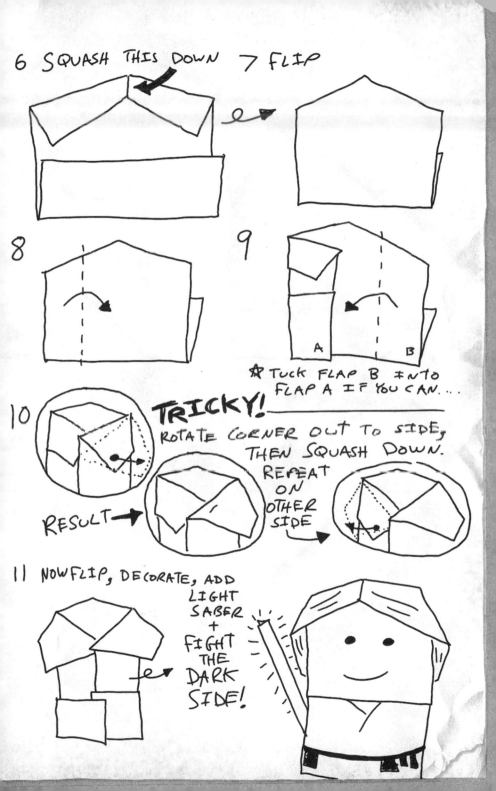

6 SQUASH THIS DOWN 7 FLIP

8

9

A   B

☆ TUCK FLAP B INTO FLAP A IF YOU CAN....

10

TRICKY!

ROTATE CORNER OUT TO SIDE, THEN SQUASH DOWN. REPEAT ON OTHER SIDE

RESULT →

11 NOW FLIP, DECORATE, ADD LIGHT SABER + FIGHT THE DARK SIDE!

ACKNOWLEDGMENTS

The list of people who make these books possible and/or better has grown longer than the books themselves!

So many people work on each book before a reader even gets to see it! There are the fantastic people at my publisher, Abrams, including Michael, Susan, Chad, Erica F., Steve, Jason, Laura, Mary, Marty, Erica W., Elisa, Alison, Jim, Scott, Chris, Jeffrey, and Melissa, who puts all the case file pieces together. Then over at Recorded Books, Mark Turetsky and the gang make an incredible audio version of the book! And other publishers and their translators let me share Dwight's story with readers in other countries!

Then there are printers, shippers, ware-housers, truckers, distributors, sales reps, and, at the end of that long chain, the booksellers, librarians, and educators, whose support for my books has just been incredible!

I wish I could mention every awesome parent, school volunteer, reading specialist, librarian, teacher, and, yes, principal who has been part of this, too! Since I can't name everyone, I'll name just one: my middle school's assistant principal, the late, great Buddy Bosserman.

Also lending a helping hand were: Brian Compton, Rocco Staino, Sketchy Steve, Ms. Rabb, Ms. Petzke, Ms. Doughty, T.J., Linda, Judy, Carla, Emily, MaryAnn, Olga, Rebecca, Charlie, Oscar, Grant, Grace, Mason, Julion, Ava, Thomas, Jack, Butch, G&KD, Sarah O'Brien, Cindy & Co., WebBuilder Gordon, Webmaster Sam, SilentMiaow, Sharp and Schu and Jonker, The Nerdy Book Club, Tina and Maria and Space Raiders, the Blacksburg UPS Store, DYMO, Excellent Table, Nest Realty, Cintiq, Barbara and George, and, of course, my parents, who are tireless supporters of me and my books.

Moral support comes from my fellow authors and illustrators, including Madelyn Rosenberg, Linda Budzinski, Ang and Tony DiTerlizzi, Michael Buckley, Amy Ignatow, Eric Wight, John Hendrix, Dan Santat, Jen Wang, T-Fed, Matthew Phelan, Brian Floca, Lisa Yee, Jon Scieszka, Michael Frye, John Rocco, Dav Pilkey, Jeff Kinney, YouKnowWho, and Michael Rex, who was nice enough to let Kellen write about Fangbone.

And then there are you folks, who actually read the books. There would have been no Origami Rebellion without you!

The SuperFolders who hang out at origamiyoda

.com are such an amazing group! But with 3,662 SF accounts on origamiyoda.com, I can't list all of you here!

These are SFs who earned a place in this book by completing certain Trials of Skill: Tucker, Zach, Plo-Koon, Kirtlan, Jaymel, Aiden, Robby, Hannah, GoldNinjaFan, Harald, Hansel, EmilyC, RockHopper, TJ, UnbeatableEthan, Liz, Drew, DarthNoah, Kenneth, DarthShredder, Megan/Phred, TylerM, JohnF, CJ, OscarU, PurseGirl, Wicket, GraphicFold, Sabermaster, LegoGabe, Landon, Hunter, NickTheBadger, HeWhoWalksTheSky, Princess, Posiedon, Pi, Cosmo, JeremySS, Michael, CadFold, LegoBuilder, FoldingTrooper, AnakinSkypaper, Stookynessman, Gavin, Luke, Captain Meatz, OdeYoda, Cameron520, Jabba, SeanSolo, YodaFett, JackF, Origamaster217, Jishua, Tanner, Markiv18, EthanDear, Grant, JC, Yodamaster, Dawson, UmHiGuy, Jedi Wookie, OrigamiLukeP100, AustinM, Carter, EvilJawa, Jessenia, Mika, WillIAmOrigami, JackF, EliGuy, 7Wonders, Nachobeans, Sophie, Kris, OrigamiMichael and his brother, Ninja, StookyLukey, Captain Ian, and all O.Y.E.U. writers and artists! And special thanks go to NathanielW, inventor of the NathanielW Base, which I used to fold the Princess for the cover of this book.

Whether you're an official SuperFolder or not, I truly appreciate everybody who, after reading one of my books, has folded, doodled, filmed, acted, sung, or written their own thing! You are stooky!

This particular book never would have existed without Carrie Fisher, Carrie Fisher's hairstylist, and all the other amazingly talented people of LucasFilm who created Princess Leia. Special thanks go to the book folks, especially Carol Roeder and Joanne Chan Taylor. And my very best wishes go to Dave Filoni and J.J. Abrams as they continue this amazing story!

None of the books would have happened without my agent, Caryn Wiseman!

And, I couldn't do much of anything without my constant collaborator, Cece Bell!

ABOUT THE AUTHOR

Tom Angleberger is the author of the *New York Times* bestselling Origami Yoda series. He is also the author of *Fake Mustache* and *Horton Halfpott*, both Edgar Award nominees, and *The Qwikpick Papers*. Tom maintains the Origami Yoda-inspired blog origamiyoda.com. He is married to author-illustrator Cece Bell and lives in Christiansburg, Virginia.

This book was designed by Melissa J. Arnst and art directed by Chad W. Beckerman. The main text is set in 10-point Lucida Sans Typewriter. The display typeface is ERASER. Tommy's comments are set in Kienan, and Harvey's comments are set in Good Dog. The hand lettering on the cover was done by Jason Rosenstock.

THE
END?